SPORTS BRANDS

UNDER ARMOUR

BY SARAH ROGGIO

Content Consultants
Dr. Antonio S. Williams
Associate Professor
Director of Sport Management
Indiana University Bloomington

Zack P. Pedersen
PhD Student
Sport Marketing and Management
Indiana University Bloomington

Essential Library

An Imprint of Abdo Publishing
abdobooks.com

ABDOBOOKS.COM

Published by Abdo Publishing, a division of ABDO, PO Box 398166, Minneapolis, Minnesota 55439. Copyright © 2023 by Abdo Consulting Group, Inc. International copyrights reserved in all countries. No part of this book may be reproduced in any form without written permission from the publisher. Essential Library™ is a trademark and logo of Abdo Publishing.

Printed in the United States of America, North Mankato, Minnesota.
052022
092022

THIS BOOK CONTAINS RECYCLED MATERIALS

Cover Photo: Tony Avelar/AP Images
Interior Photos: Thurman James/Cal Sport Media/Alamy, 4–5; Shutterstock Images, 6, 16, 31; Monkey Business Images/Shutterstock Images, 8; Zhong Fubao/Imagine China/AP Images, 11; Bill O'Leary/The Washington Post/Getty Images, 14–15; Axel Seidemann/AP Images, 20; KPA Publicity Stills/United Archives GmbH/Alamy, 24–25; Imagine China Limited/Alamy, 29; Scott Boehm/BOEHS/AP Images, 32; Joe Raymond/AP Images, 34–35; Matt Dunham/AP Images, 36, 44; Jan von Nebenan/Shutterstock Images, 38; Rob Carr/Getty Images Sport/Getty Images, 40; Olivier Douliery/AFP/Getty Images, 42; Petr David Josek/AP Images, 45; Darren Lee/Cal Sport Media/ZUMA Wire/AP Images, 46–47; Roman Tiraspolsky/Shutterstock Images, 50; Frederic Reglain/Alamy, 52; Thearon W. Henderson/Getty Images Sport/Getty Images, 57; Brien Aho/AP Images, 58–59; Russell Hons/Cal Sport Media/ZUMA Wire/AP Images, 62; Juan Lainez/Marin Media/Cal Sport Media/AP Images, 65; Kim Hairston/TNS/Newscom, 68; Postmodern Studio/Shutterstock Images, 69; Alan Warren/Houston Chronicle/The Courier/AP Images, 70–71; Adam Pantozzi/NBAE/Getty Images, 75; Yen Duong/Reuters/Alamy, 78; Larry Busacca/Getty Images Entertainment/Getty Images, 80–81; Mark Sagliocco/FilmvMagic/Getty Images, 85; Imagine China/AP Images, 87; Phelan M. Ebenhack/EBENP/AP Images, 90–91; Kevin Khoo/Shutterstock Images, 94; Tada Images/Shutterstock Images, 97; Brandon Bell/Getty Images News/Getty Images, 98

Editor: Arnold Ringstad
Series Designer: Sarah Taplin

Library of Congress Control Number: 2021951577
Publisher's Cataloging-in-Publication Data
Names: Roggio, Sarah, author.
Title: Under Armour / by Sarah Roggio.
Description: Minneapolis, Minnesota : Abdo Publishing, 2023 | Series: Sports brands | Includes online resources and index.
Identifiers: ISBN 9781532198168 (lib. bdg.) | ISBN 9781098271817 (ebook)
Subjects: LCSH: Clothing and dress--Juvenile literature. | Sport clothes industry--Juvenile literature. | Brand name products--Juvenile literature.
Classification: DDC 338.7--dc23

CONTENTS

CHAPTER ONE
UNDER ARMOUR REBOUNDS 4

CHAPTER TWO
IT STARTED WITH SWEAT 14

CHAPTER THREE
A BIG BREAK ON THE BIG SCREEN 24

CHAPTER FOUR
RISE, FALL, AND RISE AGAIN 34

CHAPTER FIVE
UNDER ARMOUR INNOVATIONS. 46

CHAPTER SIX
POWERING COLLEGE AND PRO ATHLETES 58

CHAPTER SEVEN
SUPPORTING YOUTH ATHLETES. 70

CHAPTER EIGHT
MARKETING AND MESSAGING 80

CHAPTER NINE
THE FUTURE OF UNDER ARMOUR 90

ESSENTIAL FACTS	100	INDEX	110
GLOSSARY	102	ABOUT THE AUTHOR	112
ADDITIONAL RESOURCES	104	ABOUT THE CONSULTANTS	112
SOURCE NOTES	106		

CHAPTER ONE

UNDER ARMOUR REBOUNDS

E lena took a big sip from her water bottle. Then she pushed her headband up higher above her eyes as she scanned the crowd for her family. She spotted her parents and brother. Her stomach flipped.

As she sat on the bench and waited for the game to begin, Elena was grateful that her half-zip Under Armour Velocity training top wicked away the sweat. She took some slow, deep breaths, as her coach had taught her. She felt her face grow cooler, but she couldn't stop her foot from bouncing on the boards. Today, her team was facing its archrival. She knew her family was eager to see her play. She'd been practicing all season, working toward this moment. She fiddled with her Under

> *Under Armour gear can be seen on basketball courts at every level of play.*

> *Stephen Curry's brand of basketball shoes are a key part of Under Armour's product line.*

Armour Curry Flow 8 basketball shoes, tightening up the laces one more time. The shoes' strong grip on the court gave her one less worry.

"Let's line up, Tigers!" her coach said.

The referee blew the whistle. Her teammate Kahleah won the tipoff, sending the ball to Elena. Elena bounced it once, twice, then dribbled it off her foot and out of bounds. Elena made a few shots in the first half. But after causing too many turnovers, she went into halftime feeling low. Her Tigers were down by 16.

As Elena sipped from her water bottle, she spied her parents smiling in the stands. Her brother just stuck out his tongue. She resisted the urge to respond. Elena remembered how hard she'd worked during her many hours of practice.

"Who's got this?" her coach said.

"We've got this!" Elena shouted along with her teammates.

Elena felt her focus return after this familiar routine. She tossed her training top onto her chair. Then she hustled onto the court along with her teammates. As the game continued, Elena felt her confidence growing. Dribble, drive, plant, turn, shoot. She remembered what to do and how good it felt.

Elena hit two jump shots in a row. Then she was fouled hard while driving the lane. She picked herself up off the floor and headed to the foul line. She wiped her sweaty hands on her Under Armour girls basketball shorts. With her hands now cool and dry, Elena got a good grip on the ball and made both free throws.

The Tigers' offense was starting to click, but the girl Elena was defending against, Candace, kept driving past her and scoring. In the final moments of the game, the Tigers were down by one. Candace tried to drive past Elena once again, but this time Elena was ready.

▶ *Planting the feet, making quick moves, and stopping suddenly are all common in basketball, requiring a special type of shoe designed for stability and support.*

She planted her feet, and the traction from her Curry Flow 8 shoes kept her stable. With a quick jab, she stole the ball. Then she fired the outlet pass to Kahleah, who cruised in for the game-winning layup. Elena heard her Tiger teammates roar and ran to celebrate with them. After hugs and high fives, she turned to her coach.

"I've got this!" Elena said.

"Call it a comeback!" he responded.

Later, Elena grinned as she hugged her parents.

"I wasn't sure you could pull it off," her brother said. "It looked like you were really sweating out there!"

Elena just kept on smiling. As they all stepped out into the sunshine, Elena slipped on her Under Armour Playmaker mirrored sunglasses. They defended against the sun's harmful rays—just as Elena had defended against Candace's drive. "It was no problem," Elena said. "I just kept my cool."

HELPING ATHLETES GET INTO THE FLOW

Under Armour is an American company that makes apparel, footwear, and accessories for men, women, and kids. From hats to shirts, shorts, and shoes, Under Armour provides top-to-bottom gear for athletes in a wide variety of sports. Elite athletes in sports such as baseball, basketball, and boxing have sported the Under Armour logo. Even ballerina Misty Copeland has been an Under Armour ambassador.

DESIGNED FOR FEMALE PLAYERS

In 2020, Under Armour released the first UA HOVR basketball shoes created for female athletes. All UA HOVR basketball shoes have foam cushioning designed to reduce impact and help players propel themselves forward on the court. Women's UA HOVR Breakthru basketball shoes were also designed to specifically fit and support a woman's foot.

Under Armour had female basketball players test its new sneaker while it was in development. The company sought input on the shoes from three American pros. Women's National Basketball Association (WNBA) players Bella Alarie, Tyasha "Ty" Harris, and Kaila Charles signed multiyear deals in 2020 to represent the Under Armour brand.

Under Armour's goal is to sell products that make all athletes better, whether they are pros or amateurs. Since the company was founded in 1996, it has focused on innovation to create new products. Curry Brand basketball gear is one example. The products were developed in partnership with Golden State Warriors star guard Stephen Curry. Notably, Curry Brand products feature Curry's personal logo, a level of endorsement that few athletes achieve.

Introduced in 2020, this product line offers footwear, apparel, and accessories that include Under Armour's innovations. The Curry Flow 8 basketball shoes, for example, feature the company's UA Flow technology. The sneaker's midsole is made of a proprietary foam compound that makes the shoe lightweight while also providing good traction on the court.

Under Armour has released several Curry-branded shoes

CELEBRATING BLACK BALTIMORE

The Curry Flow 8 "Beautiful Flow" basketball shoes are part of the Black History Month collection of Stephen Curry's namesake brand. These shoes were inspired by community leader and photographer Devin Allen's book *Beautiful Ghetto*, which celebrates overlooked communities in Baltimore, Maryland. The shoe incorporates the black, red, and green of the Pan-African flag. The asphalt in Baltimore's streets inspired the texture of the shoe's upper suede panel. Proceeds from sales of the shoe help support youth education programs at West Baltimore's Hilton Recreation Center.

> *Curry's longstanding involvement with the brand included helping open a new Under Armour store in Shanghai, China, in 2015.*

since Curry signed a long-term endorsement contract with the company in 2013. After testing an early version of a UA Flow sneaker in 2019, Curry told Under Armour he wanted the Curry 8 to include this technology.

UNDER ARMOUR'S COMEBACK

Under Armour got its start with clothing made from fabric designed to keep athletes comfortable in all kinds of conditions. Its product line has since grown to include the latest in technology trends, including running shoes that connect to an app that tracks athletes' runs. The company raised its profile by outfitting professional teams and signing pros as endorsers. Under Armour also sponsors a variety of youth sports.

The company has grown to be a strong competitor in the sports apparel industry. Throughout the years, Under Armour has consulted with both pro and amateur athletes to tailor its gear to meet different athletes' needs. Curry Brand continued this type of collaboration. It also represented the company's new focus after a few difficult years, including a pandemic-related downturn in sales in 2020. Like Curry returning to basketball in 2020 after missing several months because of a broken hand, Under Armour seemed to be making a comeback. In May 2021, for example,

LEGENDARY COURT REOPENED

Wilt Chamberlain, Kareem Abdul-Jabbar, and Julius Erving are among the many great basketball players who grew up playing at New York City's Holcombe Rucker Park in Harlem. Despite the park's renown for hosting both pro and playground superstars, it fell into disrepair. In October 2021, however, the park's basketball court was revitalized with new asphalt and bleachers, thanks to the National Basketball Players Association. Under Armour and its Curry Brand planned to host four youth basketball clinics each year at the park. Through a partnership with the nonprofit Good Sports, proceeds from the sales of Curry Brand apparel and footwear also provided new uniforms and equipment for six New York City youth basketball programs over three years.

Under Armour reported that its North American sales had risen 32 percent between January and March of that year.[1]

In the Under Armour 2020 annual report, chief executive officer (CEO) Patrik Frisk wrote that the company continued to face challenges, including the global pandemic. But Frisk expressed optimism about the company's future. He explained, "We are on the path to becoming a stronger brand and a better run company."[2] Over the previous two decades, Under Armour became one of the most popular sports brands in the world, and the company aimed to maintain this position in the industry.

CURRY'S DAUGHTER SEALED THE DEAL

In 2013, a few companies were fighting to get Curry to be the face of their shoe brand. Nike attempted to sign him, but a poor presentation in their meeting with Curry—including repeatedly mispronouncing his name—caused him to look elsewhere. Ultimately it was Curry's then two-year-old daughter, Riley, who reportedly made the decision for Curry to join Under Armour. In 2021, her father told NBC Sports that he asked Riley to pick her favorite shoe from the shoes he had been sent. "She didn't just go for the first one. . . . She did the first three, threw them across the room, ran over, and handed me the [Under Armour] Spawn," Curry said. "That was pretty much the end of it right there."[3]

Eight years later, the partnership was still going. Curry, who has three children, collaborated with Under Armour on the Curry Brand "Street Pack" collection. The colorful shoes were released in 2021 to celebrate *Sesame Street*'s diverse cast and inclusive storylines.

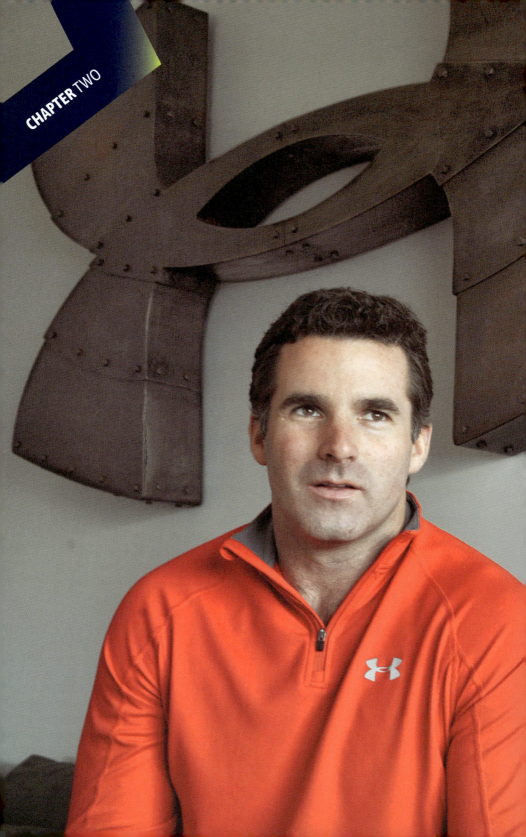

CHAPTER TWO

IT STARTED WITH SWEAT

As a high school and college football player, Kevin Plank didn't like to become sweaty. That was a problem, however. "[Plank] was the sweatiest guy on the football field," recalled high school friend Brendan Quinn. Plank hated the cotton T-shirt he wore under his uniform. He said, "It would get so wet. I changed it as often as I could."[1]

While playing college football at the University of Maryland in 1995, Plank realized that the compression shorts he wore stayed dry when his shirt got soaked. These skin-tight shorts are designed to improve athletes' performance by squeezing and supporting muscles. But it was the fabric that intrigued Plank, and that

> *Under Armour founder Kevin Plank's sports background inspired him to create the brand.*

> *Plank sought to bring the useful properties of compression shorts' fabric to other kinds of sports apparel.*

would lead him to become the founder and original CEO of Under Armour.

A SOLUTION TO SWEAT

Plank had always been interested in apparel. The compression shorts gave him the idea to create apparel that would solve the problem of too much sweat. These shorts are typically made from materials such as polyester or nylon, which wick water away from the skin and allow it to evaporate faster. For athletes, this means the body dries quickly when it sweats.

As a college senior, Plank was inspired by these shorts to create a T-shirt designed to wick away sweat. He combined cotton T-shirt material with stretchy, fast-drying fabrics used in women's lingerie. Plank created several prototypes and then asked his football teammates and other Maryland athletes to test the shirts.

"So the idea was why doesn't someone make a better alternative for a short-sleeve cotton T-shirt in the summer and a long-sleeve cotton T-shirt in the winter," Plank told the *Washington Post*. "Innovation in sports and sporting goods was limited sometimes to a shoe, every now and then to a piece of equipment, but apparel was always an afterthought, and I just wondered why. Someone had to create a better alternative."[2]

Plank graduated in 1996 with a bachelor's degree in business administration. He quickly began applying what he had learned to start growing his own business. In college he had started a business called Cupid's Valentine, which sold roses for Valentine's Day. From that company Plank earned $17,000 to invest in a new company. His first step was to have more of his sweat-wicking shirts manufactured. "I had 500 shirts made up, and I phoned every equipment manager in the

SIZING UP THE COMPETITION

In the lucrative world of sports apparel, Under Armour sits near the top of the industry. In 2019, the global sports apparel market was valued at nearly $181 billion.[3] With sales of $4.5 billion, Under Armour ranked fourth on the list that year. The industry was led by Nike at $37.4 billion. Adidas did $23.1 billion in sales, while Puma had $5.7 billion in sales. Under Armour edged out Lululemon Athletica, which had $3.8 billion in sales.[4]

[Atlantic Coast Conference] that would listen to me," Plank said, referring to the league Maryland belonged to at the time.[5] He also asked his former football teammates to help spread the word about his shirts.

THE COMPANY GETS A NAME

Plank's grandmother let him start running his business from her townhouse in Georgetown, a neighborhood in Washington, DC. He sold the shirts out of his car. Over time, his word-of-mouth efforts worked. By the end of 1996, Plank's fledgling business had managed to sell new T-shirts to Georgia Tech for its football team.

Plank's first choice for a company name was Heart, as in the saying "wearing your heart on your sleeve." His dream was denied, however, when he couldn't obtain a trademark. Plank then fell in love with the name Body Armor, but his

THE WORKOUT PROGRAM

High school football player Tyler Booker spent three years at a sports training academy in Florida before playing for the University of Alabama. His explosive play and mental strength helped him earn ESPN's top ranking for offensive tackles in the class of 2022. Booker was also selected for the inaugural year of Under Armour's athlete development program. The company launched The Workout in 2021 to help talented high school athletes prepare for a future in professional sports. The students traveled to Under Armour's Human Performance Center in Portland, Oregon, to spend four days studying topics ranging from training and recovery to personal branding.

trademark request was again denied. Plank was upset because he had already started telling people that this was going to be his new company's name.

It was a lunch with his oldest brother, Bill, that sparked a solution. Plank later told the *Washington Post* that Bill asked him, "How's that company you're working on, uhh . . . Under Armor?"[6] Plank didn't know whether his brother was teasing him, but he liked the name. Three weeks later, he got the trademark. Plank then changed Armor to the British spelling, Armour, to get what he thought would be a better toll-free phone number: 888-4ARMOUR instead of 888-44ARMOR.

PLANK'S EARLY LIFE

Kevin Plank, the youngest of five brothers, showed business skills early in life while growing up in Kensington, Maryland. In high school, Plank outearned two of his brothers while selling bracelets at a Grateful Dead concert. Plank also excelled at football at Georgetown Preparatory School, but he wasn't a great student.

In fact, Plank was expelled for getting into a brawl with Georgetown University football players. But football also set him straight. He graduated from a different high school before entering the University of Maryland and joining the football team.

GROWING PAINS

By 1997, Plank had so many orders to fill that he had to find a factory in Ohio to produce the shirts. He sold $100,000 in shirts that year, including sales from becoming the official

19

> NFL Europe, which included teams such as the Frankfurt Galaxy and the Barcelona Dragons, was an important customer in Under Armour's early years.

supplier for teams in the European pro football league, National Football League (NFL) Europe. But he had also run up $40,000 in debt using his credit cards to fund the business.[7] His friends were convinced he couldn't compete against the big players in the sports apparel industry and told him to quit. But Plank decided not to follow his friends' advice.

Plank's early business partner Kip Fulks was one of those who advised him to give up. He said Plank's motivation to continue was fueled in part by his frustration that major industry players like Nike ignored

Plank's products at industry trade shows. In fact, Plank was so confident he would succeed that he used to send Nike cofounder Phil Knight a Christmas card every year with the message, "You will know our name."[8]

Plank turned out to be right. The success of the prototype T-shirt, called the Shorty, led Plank to continue creating what would become known as performance apparel. This type of apparel uses fabrics designed to manage moisture and keep active people cool and dry.

The Shorty T-shirt was Plank's first HeatGear product. In 1997, he added to his product line with ColdGear and AllSeasonGear apparel. ColdGear fabric's goal is to keep athletes warm and dry in cold conditions, while AllSeasonGear is designed to keep athletes comfortable in changing conditions.

WORK AND PLAY

In 2016, Under Armour purchased a property intended to become the company's new Baltimore headquarters. The original plan called for housing more than 10,000 employees in four million square feet (370,000 sq m) of office space.[9] But in 2021, Under Armour announced it would be downsizing its headquarters to reflect changes that occurred during the COVID-19 pandemic in 2020, including more employees working from home.

Its new plan was to house 1,100 employees in 284,000 square feet (26,400 sq m) of office space.[10] The new campus, scheduled to open by 2025, included plans for a track-and-field facility, a multisport playing field, and basketball courts. These athletic facilities were intended for use by both Under Armour employees and the surrounding Baltimore community.

By 1998, Under Armour had made its first profit. Plank decided to move his operations out of his grandmother's basement and into new headquarters in Baltimore, Maryland, where the company has remained. Fulks became a cofounder of Under Armour and has served as the company's chief operating officer (COO) and president of product. In 2015, he became Under Armour's president of footwear and innovation.

ALLSEASONGEAR

PRODUCT SPOTLIGHT

I n 1997, Under Armour added apparel made from AllSeasonGear fabric to its product line. AllSeasonGear fabric is breathable and includes the company's Moisture Transportation technology, which helps wick sweat from athletes' bodies. The goal of this type of performance fabric is to keep athletes comfortable in the kinds of mild and changing outdoor conditions that occur in the fall. This apparel is designed to be ideal for temperatures between 55 and 75 degrees Fahrenheit (13 and 24°C).

Under Armour makes AllSeasonGear for activities such as golf, running, hiking, and hunting. AllSeasonGear apparel choices include polos, shirts, shorts, hoodies, and jackets. Under Armour also offers a line of apparel with branding from National Collegiate Athletic Association (NCAA) teams for those who want to keep comfortable while rooting for their favorite schools.

CHAPTER THREE

A BIG BREAK ON THE BIG SCREEN

In between high school and college, Plank spent a year playing football at Fork Union Military Academy in Fork Union, Virginia. His goal was to improve his chances of playing at a major college. It was this decision that helped lead to Under Armour's big break in 1999.

Plank heard from a former Fork Union football teammate that filmmaker Oliver Stone was directing a football movie called *Any Given Sunday*. Stone, a Vietnam War (1954–1975) veteran, is known for his often controversial films. These films include such titles as *Platoon* and *Born on the Fourth of July*, both of which focus on the Vietnam War. The topic of football, therefore, didn't necessarily seem to fit

> Any Given Sunday, *starring Al Pacino,* left, *and* Jamie Foxx, right, *helped put Under Armour in front of a national filmgoing audience.*

MOVIE MARKETING

Under Armour gear has been featured in a number of sports movies in addition to its big debut in the football film *Any Given Sunday*. In the 2005 baseball film *Bad News Bears*, a youth baseball team wore Under Armour uniforms and their coach, played by Greg Kinnear, had an Under Armour shirt. Baseball team members also wore Under Armour uniforms in 2014's *Million Dollar Arm*. In the 2006 movie *Gridiron Gang*, a football team and its coach, played by Dwayne "The Rock" Johnson, all sported Under Armour apparel. In the football film *The Blind Side*, released in 2009, a football team also wore Under Armour uniforms.

in with Stone's interests. But it turns out Stone had wanted to make a football movie since he was a kid watching the Baltimore Colts play in the 1950s. *Any Given Sunday* covered football controversies such as racism, greed, and medical issues.

UNDER ARMOUR'S FILM DEBUT

Whether or not Plank knew about Stone's shared interest in football or the movie's themes, he was interested in the publicity the film could provide.

The film starred famous actor Al Pacino as a coach and soon-to-be-famous actor Jamie Foxx as a quarterback. Plank sent Under Armour product samples to the film's costume designer, and the filmmakers requested a large quantity of clothing. Plank made a product placement deal, hoping to ensure that people knew Under Armour was a real, not fictional, brand.

Just as Foxx had gotten his big break in this role, Under Armour got its big break from Foxx in the film. The fictional Miami Sharks football team wore Under Armour apparel throughout the film. But it was a locker room scene in which Foxx sported a jockstrap with the Under Armour logo that brought the company the most attention.

THE WORD GETS OUT

Any Given Sunday was a box office success, grossing more than $100 million worldwide.[1] In 2000, Under Armour looked to build off this exposure. Employees volunteered to forgo their paychecks so the company could spend $25,000 on its first print ad, a half-page ad in *ESPN The Magazine*, which had a circulation of about 800,000 at that time.[2] The ad described Under Armour as "performance apparel for any given condition"

THE ROCK'S PRODUCT LINE

In 2016, actor and former professional wrestler Dwayne "The Rock" Johnson joined Under Armour's all-star roster. The company called on him to help promote its Connected Fitness apps and its UA Freedom initiative, which supported military members, public safety officials, and first responders. As part of the endorsement, Johnson has collaborated with Under Armour on footwear, apparel, and accessories. These products featured The Rock's personal logo. The first Rock-inspired items were a backpack and duffel bag, launched in 2016 at select Under Armour Brand Houses. In 2020, Under Armour introduced the Project Rock 3 training shoe, designed with an all-knit upper to provide breathability during workouts.

and touted the company's HeatGear, ColdGear, and AllSeasonGear product lines.[3]

In three weeks, the ad campaign generated $800,000 in sales. By the end of 2000, Under Armour had grown almost five times faster than in the previous year, leaping from $1.3 million in sales in 1999 to $5 million in 2000.[4] Product placement and advertising deals had paid off big time for Under Armour.

THE BIG LEAGUES

The following year, the company made the jump from the big screen to the big leagues. In 2001, Under Armour became an official supplier for the National Hockey League (NHL) and made a licensing deal with Major League Baseball (MLB). By 2003, Under Armour apparel was worn by players on 30 NFL teams, and the company had added Major League Soccer and the US Ski Team to its roster.

Under Armour's product placement in *Any Given Sunday* was also the start of an ongoing

TOM BRADY, LOYAL AMBASSADOR

Superstar NFL quarterback Tom Brady has been a loyal brand ambassador for Under Armour since 2010. His collaborations with the company include sleepwear meant to help athletes recover after workouts. Brady's overall endorsement earnings in 2021 totaled $31 million, and his Under Armour partnership made up a portion of that figure.[5] As part of his contract, Brady also became an Under Armour shareholder.

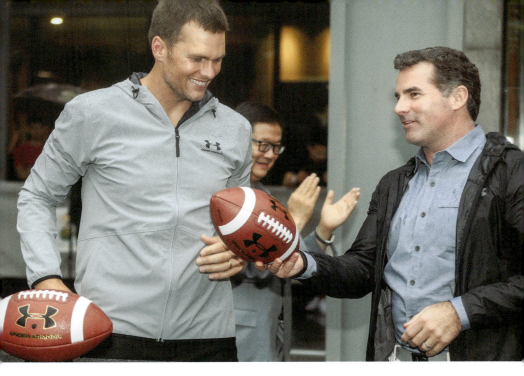

> Tom Brady and Plank open an Under Armour store in Shanghai, China, in 2017.

relationship with the entertainment world. In 2008, Under Armour hosted a star-studded gathering during the ESPY Awards, a sports award show created by the cable channel ESPN. The company also sponsored the ESPYs.

Product placement has become part of Under Armour's marketing strategy. In addition to *Any Given Sunday*, the company's apparel has appeared in numerous other Hollywood movies, including *Dodgeball*, *Superbad*, and *The Social Network*. Movie cast members have worn such Under Armour gear as skullcaps, hats, sunglasses, wristbands, T-shirts, and mock turtlenecks. Under Armour's products can be spotted on the small screen, too, ranging from the high school football team in *Friday Night Lights* to golf characters in a Tiger Woods video game.

RISING STAR

By 2002, Under Armour products were carried in 2,500 retail stores.[6] The company had exceeded $50 million in sales.[7] The next year, the company grew to $100 million in sales.[8] Accolades the company received in 2003 provided other signs that Under Armour was becoming a true contender in the sports apparel industry. In 2003, Plank won Ernst & Young's Entrepreneur of the Year award for Maryland in the manufacturing category. A 2003 issue of *Fast Company* magazine included Under Armour in its list of "Fast 50" innovative, up-and-coming companies. That same year, Under Armour was named

JORDAN SPIETH'S BIG "X"

In 2013, Under Armour expanded its presence to the golf world by signing rising star Jordan Spieth shortly after he turned pro at 19. In 2015, the year Spieth won the Masters, Under Armour extended its partnership with a ten-year deal going through 2025. The company's collaborations with Spieth have included the 2020 Spieth 4 GTX golf shoes, which feature Gore-Tex fibers to make the shoes waterproof.

During the 2021 PGA Championship, Spieth found himself facing some gentle online teasing for his apparel. The Under Armour logo on the back of his shirt was enormous. Some social media users commented that it looked as if he had an "X" target on his back.

> Under Armour's retail presence has given the company a place to connect with fans of the brand in person.

Apparel Supplier of the Year by a sporting goods industry group.

In 2005, Plank decided it was time to take Under Armour public. Going public changes a privately owned

> Under Armour gear, including cleats, has long had a place on NFL fields, and the company even became an official league partner.

venture into a publicly owned business. Investors can then buy and sell the company's stock in hopes of making money. Businesses often go public in order to raise money from investors and help the company expand. Under Armour sold 9.5 million shares of stock and ended up with net proceeds of $112.7 million as a result of going public.[9]

In 2006, Under Armour added footwear to its products, introducing its first line of football cleats and becoming the official footwear supplier to the NFL. In 2007, Under Armour opened its first Brand House retail store in Annapolis, Maryland, where the company sold its latest innovations and styles. By 2009, Under Armour had added performance training shoes and running shoes to its product line. One year later, the company eclipsed $1 billion in sales.[10] Under Armour's star was rising.

PERFORMANCE UNDERWEAR

U nder Armour refers to itself as the originator of performance apparel, and in 2002 it added its first line of performance underwear to its apparel offerings. It described this line as being "made to stretch, recover, stay put, wick sweat, and breathe." Athletes, the company said, would "never want to wear regular underwear again."[11]

In 2012, the company spent an estimated $1 million to promote its latest Boxerjock products.[12] The ad campaign featured Carolina Panthers quarterback Cam Newton, who signed with Under Armour in 2011 in what was called the biggest-ever endorsement deal for an incoming NFL rookie. In 2012, the company added the Armour Bra to its performance underwear lines. This sports bra was designed by women to better fit each woman's cup size.

CHAPTER FOUR

RISE, FALL, AND RISE AGAIN

Looking at the numbers, it may seem that Under Armour's star continued to shine throughout the 2010s. The company's annual revenue rose from $1.4 billion in 2011 to $5.2 billion in 2019.[1] But numbers don't always tell the entire story. Under Armour faced tough challenges during this period that made many people wonder what might happen to the company.

A high point of this period came in 2014, when Under Armour made what was described at the time as the largest deal in college athletics. The company entered a ten-year deal with the University of Notre Dame to be the exclusive outfitter for its 26 varsity sports teams. But that same year, an opportunity for Under Armour

> *Kevin Plank, right, appeared at a Notre Dame press conference to celebrate the 2014 deal between the brand and the school.*

The speedskating suits that Under Armour provided to the US Olympic team in 2014 proved controversial.

to gain exposure on a global level became a dent in the company's reputation. At the 2014 Winter Olympics in Sochi, Russia, the US speedskating team debuted its new Under Armour suits. When the team started to lose, some team members blamed the suits, and the team requested to switch back to its old Under Armour suits. After this news broke, Under Armour's stock decreased 2.4 percent on February 14, 2014.[2]

SALES MISSTEPS

While the Sochi speedskating suits ended up being a small speed bump, Under Armour would soon face bigger troubles closer to home. In 2017, industry analysts worried when Under Armour reported that sales in the North American market, which made up about 60 percent of the company's total sales, had declined 5 percent.[3] Analysts blamed this drop on Under Armour's unwillingness to offer the more casual type of sports clothing, known as athleisure wear, that was being made popular by companies such as Lululemon Athletica. Analysts also suggested that the company's focus on selling products in stores rather than online was a disastrous move. The CEO of retailer Dick's Sporting Goods, Ed Stack, even called out Under Armour's flooding of its stores with unpopular products as a cause of the company's revenue shortfall. By the summer of 2018, the amount of Under Armour's unsold inventory had grown 11 percent to $1.3 billion.[4]

The 2020 global pandemic hit many companies hard, and Under Armour was no

WHAT IS ATHLEISURE WEAR?

When Under Armour's sales started to slip in 2017, analysts blamed the slide in part on the company's unwillingness to adapt to athleisure wear. The term *athleisure* has come to describe athletic clothing that is both visually appealing and comfortable. This fashion trend was pioneered in the 2010s by apparel company Lululemon Athletica and popularized by women wearing yoga pants in both casual and formal settings. Other common athleisure products include leggings, sweatpants, sneakers, hoodies, and jackets. The athleisure market is estimated to reach $455 billion by 2026.[5]

> Under Armour is far smaller than its largest rival, Nike.

exception. Analysts noted that the company's lack of focus on online shopping prior to the pandemic partly contributed to its 2020 sales plunge. Under Armour's sales dropped 15 percent in 2020 to $4.5 billion.[6] Although the company's online sales grew 40 percent in 2020, that figure paled in comparison with Nike, which saw a 74 percent increase in online sales that year.[7]

POOR PUBLICITY

Under Armour has faced controversy. In 2018, the *Wall Street Journal* reported that until that year, Under Armour had often footed the bill when executives and employees took athletes and colleagues to strip clubs. Although Under Armour put a stop to this practice, the company's troubles continued.

In 2019, Under Armour confirmed that the US Justice Department and the Securities and Exchange Commission (SEC) were investigating the company's accounting practices. The SEC claimed that Under Armour had misled investors in 2015 and 2016 when it asked retailers to take their orders early so Under Armour could report a predicted sales increase to investors earlier in the year. In 2021, Under Armour agreed to pay a $9 million penalty without denying or admitting to the SEC's findings.[8] The SEC noted that Under Armour had agreed to stop this practice. In 2021, a judge also decided that a related class-action lawsuit, which had been filed in 2019 to address investors' concerns about this accounting practice, could proceed.

The *New York Times* reported in 2020 that the company's troubles had also nearly included losing its partnership with Curry in 2018. He was reportedly unhappy about the sales of his Curry 3 shoe and Plank's praise of President Donald Trump. Meanwhile, Plank reportedly thought the company's star wasn't wearing enough Under Armour gear at NBA games. But in 2018,

> *Plank watched Curry play in a 2017 game in Washington, DC.*

Curry and Under Armour executives met and resolved their differences.

CHANGE IN LEADERSHIP

After founding the company and serving as its CEO for 23 years, Plank stepped down as CEO in 2020. He remained the executive chairman and brand chief of the company. He was replaced in the CEO role by former Under Armour COO Patrik Frisk.

In 2017, in his role as COO, Frisk had been tasked with stabilizing Under Armour's business and reversing its slide in sales, especially in North America. He led a three-year restructuring plan designed to cut costs and make Under

Armour more efficient. The changes included launching new products faster and selling fewer individual products. This would allow the company to coordinate with fewer factories and retailers.

In 2018, Frisk made it clear that despite analysts' concerns, Under Armour was going to stick with innovations focused on athletic activity rather than switch its focus to athleisure wear. He told investors that the company's market research showed it should still target "focused performers" who want to improve their athletic performance. In 2018, the company noted that this group of customers represented a $29 billion market in the United States and Canada, accounting for 30 percent of the athletic apparel and footwear market in North America.[9]

PATRIK FRISK

Patrik Frisk became Under Armour's CEO in 2020 after Plank stepped down as CEO. Frisk had joined the company in 2017 as its COO after spending nearly 30 years in the apparel, footwear, and retail industry. Prior to Under Armour, Frisk served as CEO of global footwear company the Aldo Group. Before Aldo, he was responsible for the North Face, Timberland, JanSport, Lucy, and Smartwool brands for apparel and footwear company VF Corporation. When he became CEO of Under Armour, Frisk said, "I joined Under Armour to be part of an iconic brand that demonstrated the power of sport and premium experience, when properly harnessed, is capable of unlimited possibilities."[10]

▶ *Frisk took over as Under Armour CEO in 2020.*

"THE ONLY WAY IS THROUGH"

In 2020, Under Armour launched an ad campaign with the slogan "The Only Way Is Through," designed to inspire all athletes to push themselves. In the 2020 Under Armour annual report, Frisk described this as the company's attitude while facing the challenges of the global pandemic. Under Armour had seen some success with its restructuring plan, including an increase in footwear sales. But then the pandemic hit the company hard. Frisk told employees in September 2020 that the company would be laying off 600 people. This represented about 3.5 percent of its workforce.[11]

Under Armour continued its restructuring plans during 2020, including selling off health apps, such as

MyFitnessPal, that it had spent millions to acquire. Under Armour had bought MyFitnessPal in 2015 for $475 million, but then sold it at a discount for $345 million. It also ended its Endomondo platform, which it had acquired for $85 million.[12] Under Armour held on to the MapMyFitness platform, which uses apps to track workouts through connected footwear.

Despite the challenges of 2020, Under Armour also showed signs of recovery and growth. It relaunched its North American online shopping platform in 2020, and then reported in the spring of 2021 that online sales were up 69 percent. Under Armour also reported that its North American store sales were up 32 percent.[13]

PANDEMIC AID

In 2020, Under Armour applied its advertising slogan, "The Only Way Is Through," to helping communities during the global pandemic. It donated $1 million to Feeding America to support hunger relief efforts related to the pandemic. To help people stay physically active during a time when many did work and schooling at home, Under Armour hosted a 30-day Healthy at Home fitness challenge through its health apps. The company also donated more than 35,000 UA Sports Masks to youth athletes to help prevent the spread of the virus while training.[14]

SPORTS FOCUS

SPEEDSKATING SUITS REBUILT

Under Armour had been supplying the US speedskating team with suits for four years when it tapped aerospace company Lockheed Martin to help create new suits for the 2014 Winter Olympics in Sochi. Working with Lockheed Martin engineers and using the aerospace company's wind tunnel facilities to test how air flows around skaters, Under Armour designed the Mach 39. The new suits featured back air vents designed to release heat and improve aerodynamics.

> *A test of a prototype speedskating suit for the 2014 Winter Olympics*

> *US speedskaters won a bronze medal in 2018 while wearing Under Armour's redesigned suits.*

But when the US speedskating team started underperforming in Sochi, some people suggested the Mach 39 was the cause. They suggested that the new vents actually hurt skaters' aerodynamics. But the story didn't end in 2014. Under Armour was given a second chance when it signed an eight-year contract that included designing new speedskating suits for the 2018 Winter Olympics in Pyeongchang, South Korea. Although US Speedskating never officially blamed Under Armour for the 2014 results, the company was determined to make things right.

It devoted many employees and hours to studying skaters' training routines and movements as part of its research. For the 2018 Mach 39, Under Armour removed the vents and added H1, a new type of fabric it described as the most aerodynamic fabric it had ever made. In Pyeongchang, the US women won a bronze medal in the team pursuit event. It marked the first Olympic medal for the US women in the sport since 2002.

CHAPTER FIVE

UNDER ARMOUR INNOVATIONS

Throughout its history, Under Armour's goal has always been innovation. Frisk made it clear in Under Armour's 2020 annual report that this will remain the company's focus into the future. He pointed to recent new products, including the UA Sports Mask, the Infinity sports bra, and the soft but still sweat-wicking Meridian women's pants. "Any product or experience we bring to market must make athletes better," Frisk explained.[1]

Fabric was the initial focus of Under Armour's innovative efforts. The company's first product, the Shorty sweat-wicking T-shirt, was the company's answer to what Plank saw as a need for athletes to have an alternative to sweat-soaked cotton shirts. Plank spent

> *Like many other apparel companies, Under Armour introduced a face mask during the COVID-19 pandemic.*

a year seeking out and testing fabric to produce the samples that would convince his first customers at Georgia Tech to buy his shirts in 1996.

HEATGEAR TECHNOLOGY

The Shorty T-shirt was Under Armour's first example of HeatGear technology. Introduced in 1996, HeatGear is a microfiber blend designed to be worn in warm temperatures to wick moisture from the body to keep athletes cool and dry. Under Armour also promoted the light weight of this fabric, saying that a regular sweat-soaked T-shirt can weigh up to three pounds (1.4 kg). Expansions to this product line have included HeatGear Armour, a stretchy material with tiny vents designed to improve breathability. Today, consumers can find HeatGear technology in Under Armour tops, bottoms, and accessories such as socks.

"By the end of the first day, we had guys [from the football team] wearing sizes they couldn't even fit in because they wanted to wear it so badly," said Georgia Tech equipment director Tom Conner.[2] It was this kind of enthusiasm that fueled Plank's anti-cotton crusade, leading to the addition of the company's ColdGear and AllSeasonGear performance apparel in 1997. In 2011, Under Armour apparently declared somewhat of a truce in what it called a "war on cotton" by creating Charged Cotton, a fabric that feels as soft as cotton but dries faster than regular cotton.

A FOOTHOLD IN FOOTWEAR

After focusing its first few years on performance apparel, Under Armour launched a line of performance training shoes in 2008. The Prototype cross-trainers included what Plank called "directional cushioning," which put padding where athletes' feet most need it.[3] These sneakers marked Under Armour's first effort to challenge the competition more directly in the athletic footwear category. Up until this point, Under Armour's footwear product line had consisted primarily of football and baseball cleats.

Under Armour kicked off its challenge by spending more than $5 million on a 60-second Super Bowl ad introducing its new shoes.[4] The ad featured a computer-generated version of Under Armour spokesman and former NFL player Eric Ogbogu, known as Big E.

COLDGEAR TECHNOLOGY

Introduced in 1997, ColdGear uses double-layer fabric to circulate body heat while wicking moisture from athletes' skin. ColdGear apparel is designed to be a light layer worn beneath uniforms, jerseys, or ski vests. In 2013, Under Armour added ColdGear Infrared to this product line. The company described this technology as a soft lining that retains body heat to help athletes stay warm without the fabric adding extra weight. In 2021, Under Armour introduced the ColdGear Infrared thermal jacket with UA Storm water-repellent technology, aimed at keeping golfers warm and dry even in cold and wet conditions.

> By the end of the first decade of the 2000s, shoes were becoming a more important part of Under Armour's product offerings.

The ad showed people working out in the company's new Prototype cross-trainer shoes. The New York Giants' Brandon Jacobs, the San Francisco 49ers' Vernon Davis, and the Chicago Cubs' Alfonso Soriano were also featured in the ad.

In 2009, Under Armour added its first performance running shoes, UA Run footwear. The shoes included the company's proprietary Cartilage technology, designed to provide more stability by better connecting a runner to the running surface. Under Armour ran several ads on MTV, ESPN, and NFL Network to introduce these shoes.

INNOVATION PARTNERS

Innovation takes work, and Under Armour has occasionally called on partners to help with this process. The company's first call for help came when Plank was trying to come up with a prototype for his new T-shirt while at the University of Maryland. He went to a nearby tailor shop to look at the available synthetic materials. Then he spent $500 to make seven different prototype shirts before he found the one he liked. "It was really that easy. I think sometimes entrepreneurs can get caught up with theorizing, hypothesizing, business planning— at some point . . . go do something," Plank told the *Washington Post*.[5]

In 2014 and 2018, when Under Armour worked with Lockheed Martin to develop the US Olympic speedskating suits, the innovation process was a much bigger undertaking. For the ill-fated Mach 39 suits from 2014, the partners created six mannequins mimicking different skaters' body positions to test in Lockheed Martin's wind

> *An example of an Under Armour 3D printed sneaker was put on display at a French museum.*

tunnels. The team also tested more than 100 textiles, including 250 different variations on zippers, seams, and fabrics. The partners' effort to redesign the 2018 suits while supporting the US team involved 56 employees. These workers spent thousands of hours studying skaters' sleep and nutrition habits in addition to studying mechanical issues involved with the suit design.

TWEAKING SNEAKERS

In 2016, Under Armour used Autodesk Within design software to create its ArchiTech trainer, the first 3D printed sneaker available to the public. Under Armour used the software to design a lattice midsole aimed at making the sneaker stable enough for weightlifting but flexible enough for cross-training. For its twentieth anniversary in 2016, Under Armour released 96 pairs of the shoes in honor of the company's start in 1996. In 2017, Under Armour added the ArchiTech Futurist sneaker to its limited-release 3D printed collection. The company built on its lattice system by adding an external sleeve designed to make the sneaker more supportive and secure.

INNOVATION LAB

In 2016, Under Armour opened a facility called the Lighthouse at its Baltimore headquarters. This space was created for employees to design and test new products to help Under Armour achieve its innovation goals. That same year, Under Armour created the components of its first connected shoe, the UA SpeedForm Gemini 2 Record Equipped, at this facility. In 2017, Under Armour used the facility to manufacture its first made-in-America apparel, a limited release of 2,000 bras and leggings.

When Under Armour created the UA HOVR sneaker in 2018, it turned to Dow Chemical to provide the proprietary cushioning foam compound for the sneaker's midsole. Then Under Armour told Dow Chemical it was interested in a lightweight foam that the company was developing. The partners took three years to conduct several rounds of raw material testing, biomechanical testing, and shoe testing.

They also had more than 130 elite athletes run more than 11,000 miles (17,700 km) to test the shoes.[6] The result was UA Flow, a grippy, supportive foam compound that eliminated a sneaker's traditional rubber outsole. Under Armour initially wanted to use UA Flow in a running shoe. But when Curry was given the chance in 2019 to test an early version of the shoe, he realized how much traction it provided on hardwood. "[Curry] ran around the practice facility . . . and one of the first things he said was, 'Man, I feel like a ninja,'" recalled Tom Luedecke, a shoe designer for Under Armour.[7] Curry then

POP-UP PERFORMANCE LAB

Elite athletes can get a sneak peek of Under Armour's latest technology at the company's headquarters. But sometimes Under Armour brings its newest innovations to the public. In 2019, during a pop-up performance lab event in New York City, Under Armour unveiled its UA Rush product line of tops and bottoms.

Under Armour partnered with technology company Celliant to create the new fabric. It contains minerals designed to absorb heat given off during exercise. The pop-up event included a promotional video featuring Under Armour endorsers such as Curry and Kelley O'Hara, a star defender for the US women's soccer team.

54

CONNECTED FOOTWEAR

PRODUCT SPOTLIGHT

In 2016, Under Armour released its first version of connected footwear, shoes that digitally track athletes' performance. The UA SpeedForm Gemini 2 Record Equipped sneaker contained Record Sensor technology that allowed runners to track such data as date, duration, and distance of a run.

The company expanded its data-tracking capabilities in 2018 by adding a sensor to the midsole of its UA HOVR shoes. The sensor connects to the MapMyRun app via Bluetooth wireless technology. Under Armour promoted this new product as providing "personalized coaching" that includes such detailed data as pace and stride length.[8]

To track this data, athletes open the app when they are near the shoes and then pair the sensor with the app. If athletes are running without a phone, the tracked data automatically syncs with the app once the shoes come close to a runner's mobile device.

In 2019, Under Armour added Gait Coaching, which provides a stride-by-stride analysis of an athlete's run. It also provides historical running data to help athletes see if they are improving with each run. By 2021, runners had linked more than one million pairs of Under Armour connected shoes to the MapMyRun app.[9]

convinced the company to add it to his Curry Flow 8 sneakers, which were launched in 2020.

In 2021, Under Armour introduced this foam compound to the running community by releasing the UA Flow Velociti Wind. The company's goal was to create a lightweight running shoe, and by eliminating the midsole it had removed up to three ounces (85 g) of weight. Under Armour also touted athletes' ability to run with confidence on surfaces ranging from uneven gravel to wet pavement because of the traction the shoes provide.

During its annual shareholders meeting in 2021, Frisk said the Velociti Wind had helped elevate the HOVR footwear line to a more premium position. Company officials also pointed to footwear as one of the company's opportunities for future growth. During the meeting, Frisk restated that the company's future focus will remain the same as it had always been: on innovation.

Stephen Curry runs up the court in his signature Under Armour shoes made with UA Flow technology.

CHAPTER SIX

POWERING COLLEGE AND PRO ATHLETES

Selling college and pro athletes on the benefits of its innovative products has been a big part of Under Armour's strategy since the beginning. After snagging its first customer, Georgia Tech, in 1996, Under Armour's next notable collegiate collaboration occurred in 2004. Plank returned to his alma mater, the University of Maryland, where he had first conceived of his company. Under Armour then struck a deal with the university to become the official supplier for its athletic teams.

In 2014, Under Armour and the university further cemented their relationship with a ten-year, nearly $33 million contract for athletic apparel and rights fees. As part of this deal, Under

> *Under Armour began outfitting the athletic teams of the University of Maryland in 2004.*

NATASHA HASTINGS FOUNDATION

Natasha Hastings, the two-time Olympic gold medalist and five-time world champion sprinter, has had the help of Under Armour human performance experts since 2017 to get her body in the best shape for competition. But in 2019, when she struggled to find a Black therapist to help support her as a newly single mother, she realized how much mental well-being was stigmatized in the Black and athletic communities.

She established the Natasha Hastings Foundation, which aims to empower girls to become confident women in sports and life. Hastings said, "When I was signed to Under Armour, a woman signed me. When I made the call to Under Armour to tell them I was pregnant, I made that call to a woman. It's important for women to be telling our stories and making decisions for us. A lot of times, women are left out of the conversation because the people making the decisions don't look like us, don't understand us."[3]

Armour promised the university up to $1.8 million in Under Armour products, ranging from specialty gear for athletes to polo shirts and T-shirts for coaches and staff.[1]

EXTENDED DEALS

In 2019, while Under Armour was restructuring itself, the company confirmed it would be sticking with its commitment to the University of Maryland. That same year, Plank donated $25 million to a $210 million renovation of the university's Cole Field House.[2] The plans included locker rooms, weight rooms, dining areas, offices, meeting space, and two Bermuda-grass practice fields for the Terps football team.

In 2021, Under Armour announced that it was also extending its partnership with the University of Minnesota

Duluth. The company had become the official outfitter of the university in 2013. In the new deal, Under Armour promised to continue providing training and competition gear for the university's varsity teams through 2028. The company would also provide Under Armour apparel for coaches and staff.

DROPPED SPONSORSHIPS

Although some universities forged continuing partnerships with Under Armour, other deals did not make the cut. In fact, the company reduced its sponsorships by 47 percent in 2020 as part of its cost-cutting efforts during the global pandemic.[4] Under Armour also renegotiated marketing contracts with some of its elite sponsored athletes to delay payments as part of a $325 million reduction in operating costs.[5]

ENDORSEMENT: BRYCE HARPER

In 2016, Under Armour entered a ten-year extension of its endorsement agreement with Philadelphia Phillies right fielder Bryce Harper. The agreement was reported to be the largest endorsement deal ever offered to an MLB player. Under Armour first signed Harper in 2011, less than a year after he was the number one MLB Draft pick by the Washington Nationals. As part of this partnership, Under Armour has collaborated with the two-time National League Most Valuable Player Award winner to create several Harper-branded baseball cleats. This includes the UA Harper 6 Low ST baseball cleats, which feature UA HOVR cushioning technology and the new, lighter UA MicroTips spikes.

> *Under Armour has had a longstanding relationship with the University of Minnesota Duluth.*

Prior to the pandemic, as part of its restructuring efforts, Under Armour had already started dropping out of existing deals. In 2018, Under Armour exited a deal it had made with MLB in 2016 to start supplying all on-field jerseys. The move reportedly saved the company nearly $50 million.[6] Under Armour's cost cutting continued into 2021, when the company ended its NFL on-field licensing contract just days before the Super Bowl.

The move restricted players, including star quarterback and key Under Armour endorser Tom Brady, from wearing accessories bearing the Under Armour logo on the field during games. Estimated at between $10 million and $15 million per year, the contract primarily covered such products as gloves as well as apparel that college prospects wear for the NFL's annual Scouting Combine workouts in Indianapolis, Indiana.[7]

COLLEGIATE COLLAPSES

Pros weren't the only players that Under Armour said no to during this period. In 2020, Under Armour reached a deal with the University of Cincinnati to exit its $50 million partnership. The buyout agreement required Under Armour to provide $3.65 million worth of product to the university through

SHOES WITH A MESSAGE

In 2019, Liverpool and England soccer star Trent Alexander-Arnold signed a four-year extension to his Under Armour contract, reported to be worth £6.4 million, or about $8.6 million in US dollars. Alexander-Arnold was reportedly earning £1.6 million per year, or about $2.1 million in US dollars, making the deal one of the biggest shoe contracts in English soccer.[8] As part of his partnership with Under Armour, Alexander-Arnold has used his shoes to raise awareness about issues important to him.

In 2020, he wore Black Lives Matter shoes to speak out against racism and police brutality against Black people. In October 2021, during Breast Cancer Awareness Month, he wore pink shoes with the names of his two aunts, Cathy and Carmen, to honor them as breast cancer survivors. "Family is everything, but cancer brought our family even closer together. And we know how lucky we are to still have my aunties with us," Alexander-Arnold said.[9]

June 2021. Under Armour also had to pay the university a $9.75 million exit fee.[10]

Under Armour had been the university's official outfitter since 2015. This partnership was part of a ten-year agreement that was reportedly one of the 20 most lucrative deals in college sports. But the ending of this deal was not a complete breakup. As part of the negotiations, the university can buy Under Armour apparel at a discount through BSN Sports, a distributor of team apparel and equipment. Under Armour will also still pay the university bonuses if its teams perform well, such as $100,000 if the football team wins a national championship.[11]

The ending of Under Armour's relationship with the University of California, Berkeley, did not go as smoothly. As part of the deal it had struck with the university in 2016, Under Armour had agreed to design and supply footwear, apparel, and equipment for Cal's teams. In 2020, the company sought to end the deal, which was set to expire in 2027. Cal disagreed with Under Armour's claim that it had a right to prematurely terminate the deal. But it was later reported that the agreement had ended.

> Before UCLA's contentious split with Under Armour, the brand's logos could be seen widely along the team's sideline.

BITTER BREAKUP

Under Armour had an especially bitter breakup with the University of California, Los Angeles (UCLA). In 2020, UCLA filed a lawsuit against Under Armour when the company tried to terminate what had been a record-breaking $280 million sponsorship deal signed in 2016.[12] This 15-year agreement had terms similar to Under Armour's deal with Cal, including varsity team apparel as well as internship and employment opportunities. In seeking to end the partnership, Under Armour tried to use one of the same reasons it had given Cal, saying that the pandemic was an extraordinary circumstance that freed both parties from their contractual obligations. UCLA disagreed, filing a lawsuit in 2020. Under Armour filed a countersuit in 2021 to try to get the UCLA suit dismissed.

It claimed UCLA had ignored its request in 2020 to have its teams place a new social justice "Stand Together" patch somewhere else than over Under Armour's logo. UCLA disagreed with this claim as well, and a judge decided in 2021 that Under Armour could not get the case dismissed. The case worked its way through the courts in 2021. In the meantime, UCLA signed a deal

COLLEGE SOFTBALL STARS SIGNED

College softball stars Rachel Garcia and Odicci Alexander signed endorsement deals with Under Armour in 2021. Garcia, a 2020 Olympic silver medalist, helped guide the UCLA Bruins to a 2019 NCAA championship. She was also honored as a top US female collegiate athlete with the Honda Cup and Collegiate Woman of the Year awards.

During the 2021 Women's College World Series, Alexander helped her team reach the semifinals. She amazed fans when she jumped into the air to make a run-saving tag at the plate. These women became the second and third Under Armour softball signees, joining Cat Osterman, who signed with Under Armour in 2007.

with Nike to supply apparel to 22 of the school's 25 varsity teams through 2026.[13]

Despite the challenges involved with ending some of its sponsorships, Frisk said at Under Armour's 2021 annual shareholders meeting that the company was ready to make new deals again, including with college athletes. Frisk told Yahoo! Finance that he saw many opportunities after a 2021 NCAA rule change allowed college athletes to benefit financially from their name, image, and likeness. He said work will need to be done to ensure that companies, athletes, and universities all benefit. "There's a lot of cooperation that's needed to help these very young people . . . navigate this," Frisk said.[14]

SPORTS FOCUS

HOVR TECHNOLOGY

When Under Armour was looking for a way to compete in the running shoe market, it turned to Dow Chemical for an edge. At the time, most major shoe brands were moving away from using the standard ethylene-vinyl acetate (EVA) as their midsole material because runners complained that the material lost its bounce with long-term use. With Dow's help, Under Armour soon followed suit.

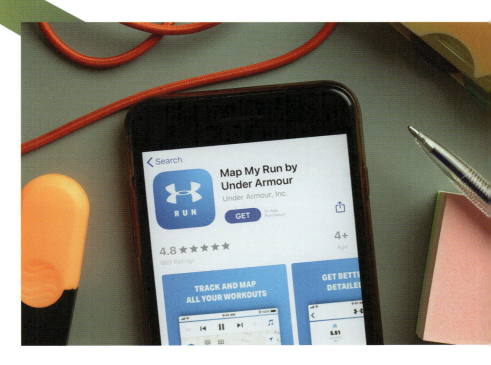

In 2018, the company released the UA HOVR sneaker, featuring a new type of cushioning midsole made from a proprietary foam compound. The company also touted what it called the shoe's Energy Web, a mesh fabric wrapped around the cushioning core designed to absorb the impact of runners' steps and help them feel less fatigued.

In 2018, Under Armour connected its UA HOVR shoes to its MapMyRun app, which tracks runners' data. In 2020, the company added the UA HOVR Machina. This sole of this sneaker features a "propulsion plate" made from Pebax, a polymer created by the chemical company Arkema and used by many sports brands. The company also added real-time coaching to its MapMyRun app to help athletes improve their form as they run.

> *Under Armour chief design officer Dave Dombrow shows off two models of HOVR sneakers.*

CHAPTER SEVEN

SUPPORTING YOUTH ATHLETES

Although Under Armour's pros get most of the public attention, the company has also devoted time and resources to helping youth athletes. One of Under Armour's longest collaborations has been with the Cal Ripken Sr. Foundation. The partnership celebrated its twentieth anniversary in 2021.

The organization was founded in 2001 by brothers Bill and Cal Ripken Jr. to honor their father's devotion to coaching baseball. Cal Ripken Jr., who was inducted into the National Baseball Hall of Fame in 2007, is also known for his devotion to the sport. In 1998, as a shortstop for the Baltimore Orioles, he set a record by playing 2,632 consecutive games. Bill Ripken also played in MLB and

> *Baseball legend Cal Ripken Jr. has a longstanding connection with Under Armour's charitable efforts.*

later became an Emmy Award–winning analyst for the MLB Network.

SCORING A RUN FOR YOUTH SPORTS

Troy Grimes, an Under Armour retail employee and baseball fan, decided to celebrate his fifty-eighth birthday in 2021 by running 58 miles (93 km) to raise funds for youth sports. His goal was to raise $5,800 for Under Armour community partner Every Kid Sports, which helps kids from income-restricted families play sports by covering a portion of their registration fees.[2]

To complete his goal, Grimes signed up to run 177 laps in the Hot Rod Ultra Marathon, held at the Hot Rod Minor League Baseball field in Bowling Green, Kentucky. "I am so excited that I am able to combine my love of baseball and running with the Hot Rod Ultra Marathon. As a father and fan of sports, I have first-hand experience seeing the positive impact that youth sports can have on young kids, which is why I am honored to be raising money for Every Kids Sports," Grimes explained.[3]

The goal of the Cal Ripken Sr. Foundation is to strengthen underserved communities, which includes providing parks where kids can play safely. In 2009, Under Armour joined this mission as the foundation's first corporate partner. "Our relationship began on the youth baseball side, but like so many partners, the UA team saw the work we were doing in underserved communities and wanted to be a part of it in a significant way," said Cal Ripken Jr.[1]

As part of this partnership, Under Armour has donated more than 100,000 products, including T-shirts, shorts, socks, and backpacks, to outfit kids for the foundation's annual youth programs, summer camps, and clinics. Under Armour has also helped the foundation fund ten new youth parks across the United States, including the organization's fiftieth park, located in Chicago, Illinois. The parks have provided clean, safe places for more than 25,000 youths to play. Through its UA Freedom initiative, which supports veterans and first responders, the company has also helped with the foundation's community enhancement projects.

SAFE PLACES TO PLAY

Under Armour has also collaborated with ESPN to provide safe places for kids to play. In 2020, for the third year in a row, ESPN and Under Armour joined forces with the

YOUTH ATHLETES "READY FOR ANYTHING"

During the 2020 global pandemic, safety took on a new meaning as people had to learn how to socially distance from each other to avoid spreading COVID-19. To help high school athletes who were forced to distance from schools and coaches, Under Armour created the "Ready for Anything" online training program. Under Armour based the six-week program on athletic and strength conditioning principles that its Human Performance team uses with its elite athlete endorsers.

These athletes included Curry, sprinter Natasha Hastings, British boxer Anthony Joshua, and French Olympic judo champion Teddy Riner. "We know this is an incredibly difficult time for athletes everywhere . . . our athletes, from Olympic hopefuls to youth competitors, have consistently asked for tools to help them stay at the top of their game. This training . . . is one way Under Armour is supporting our high school student athletes," explained Paul Winsper, Under Armour's vice president of Human Performance, Science, and Research.[4]

Local Initiatives Support Corporation to fund grants to revitalize vacant spaces through the RePlay initiative. This program transforms vacant lots into community spaces for youth sports and recreation.

RePlay gives communities $10,000 planning grants and $75,000 implementation grants. In 2020, Under Armour and ESPN awarded grants to help rejuvenate vacant spaces in Milwaukee, Wisconsin; Flint, Michigan; Newark, New Jersey; and Cincinnati, Ohio. "We are honored . . . to extend the reach and impact of RePlay with the goal of increasing neighborhood access for more young people to have safe and inspiring places to play," said Stacey Ullrich, head of Global Community Impact for Under Armour.[5]

WINNING AWARDS

In 2019, ESPN recognized Under Armour's efforts to support youths and communities with its Humanitarian Corporate Community Impact Award. This award recognizes athletes, teams, and sports industry professionals who work to make a difference through sports. Under Armour received the award for its involvement in the Building Bridges through Basketball (BBTB) program. Through its UA Freedom initiative, Under

> *The Los Angeles Lakers hosted a 2017 basketball clinic as part of the Building Bridges through Basketball program, which works to build trust between young people and police.*

Armour collaborated with the NBA and the Ross Initiative in Sports for Equality (RISE) to support this program.

Launched in Chicago in 2016, BBTB is a ten-week program that aims to build trust and bridge divisions in neighborhoods by bringing together young people and members of law enforcement. The 2.5-hour sessions combine on-court basketball training and RISE leadership activities focused on diversity, identity, and conflict resolution.

Local organizations such as the Union League Boys and Girls Club in Chicago and the Naomi Drenan Recreation Center in Charlotte, North Carolina, host the sessions. "It helped me break that cycle . . . it made me start trusting the officers more, because I had something against police before all of this because of the things I've experienced," said Destiny, a 2019 BBTB youth participant.[6]

Luis Crespo, a Chicago Police Department veteran of more than two decades who began focusing on community policing in 2017, also touted the program's benefits. "It's just the idea of being part of something bigger than yourself, the idea of working with people who may be a little apprehensive to work with police and then just realize that officers are just like every individual," Crespo said.[7]

SPORTS AND EQUITY

Another way in which Under Armour is working to serve youth is to help girls find more opportunities to play sports. In honor of the annual March celebration of Women's History Month, Under Armour released its Women's History Month collections in 2020 and 2021 to support this effort. The company noted that high school sports opportunities for boys vastly outnumber those for girls.

To help address this disparity, Under Armour announced that proceeds from the collection, which included shirts and shoes, would be used to help fund two programs that support female athletes. One program is Good Sports' She Who Plays initiative, which is a commitment to provide $1 million in new sports and fitness equipment for girls in athletics.[8] Since partnering with this initiative in 2014, Under Armour has provided nearly 185,000 pieces of apparel, equipment, and footwear to programs serving 1.5 million children in all 50 states.[9]

The second program is the Girls Opportunity Alliance, led by former First Lady Michelle Obama. This program seeks to empower girls around the world through education. Under Armour wants this empowerment to extend to its own future female employees. This includes a partnership with the Women in Sports and Events organization, which focuses on advancing women to leadership roles in the sports industry. Under Armour noted that 96 percent of female high-level executives played sports beyond elementary school, including many female senior leaders at Under

SUPPORTING GIRLS' FOOTBALL

Under Armour and the Baltimore Ravens partnered to provide a high school girls' flag football program by fall of 2022 in Maryland. The Ravens committed $250,000 to the initiative, while Under Armour said it would supply custom uniforms for the teams. "At Under Armour, we believe everyone should have the opportunity and ability to play sports at every level, particularly young girls whose confidence can be impacted by lack of access to sport," said Under Armour executive Sean Eggert.[10]

> *Michelle Obama met with girls at a school in Vietnam for a Girls Opportunity Alliance event in 2019.*

Armour. "We will continue to elevate, create opportunities and open doors for women to be able to grow into higher levels of our company," said Under Armour executive Stephanie Pugliese.[11]

VETERAN YOUTH MENTORS

Under Armour has also worked to help kids both on and off the field through the Character Does Matter program of the Travis Manion Foundation (TMF). The program is powered by the UA Freedom initiative. It has connected more than 2,000 military veterans, acting as mentors, with more than 400,000 kids across the United States since 2019.[12]

The program provides veteran mentors with TMF training and materials so they can offer free character curriculum to teams, schools, and youth groups. The TMF was created in honor of Travis Manion, a US Marine who died during combat in Iraq in 2007 and was posthumously awarded a Silver Star and Bronze Star with valor. To support the foundation, actor Dwayne "The Rock" Johnson and Under Armour released a 2021 collection under the Project Rock brand called For the Heroes. This initiative was meant to honor the service and sacrifice of military veterans.

MOTIVATING YOUTH ATHLETES TO MOVE

To motivate kids to stay active and healthy, Under Armour launched the UA Next platform in 2021. The company noted that it wanted to educate and empower all kids to keep moving during a time that fitness experts have described as "an inactivity pandemic," due to such factors as schools lacking physical education programs and children pursuing more sedentary activities such as video gaming.

The UA Next platform provides a central place for youth athletes to search for annual leagues, tournaments, camps, and clinics for their sport. The UA Next Instagram feed shows kids staying active in a variety of ways. Kids are pictured pursuing traditional youth sports, such as basketball and volleyball, as well as activities such as skateboarding and dance. Under Armour planned to add tips from top coaches and trainers to the UA Next platform in 2022.

CHAPTER EIGHT

MARKETING AND MESSAGING

U nder Armour debuted its first national advertising campaign in 2003 with a 90-second football-focused television spot titled "Protect This House." The ad starred Dallas Cowboys linebacker Eric Ogbogu, who had played alongside Plank at the University of Maryland. At the time, Under Armour had little advertising money to spend, so Plank called in favors from other former Maryland football players to fill out the scenes.

The ad showed grunting players training with weights, followed by Ogbogu leading the players in a call-and-response chant. "Will you protect this house?" Ogbogu yells, after which the players shout, "I will! I will!"[1] When late-night TV talk show host

Ogbogu became the face of one of Under Armour's earliest advertising campaigns.

81

AJ'S "AMBITION"

British heavyweight champion Anthony Joshua, or AJ, is a long-term Under Armour endorser. He has collaborated with the company through his personal brand, AJBXNG. These efforts have included testing a new type of boxing boot made from a "second skin" material designed to move with the body. AJ has also shared his mental training advice for all athletes through the UA Performance Academy, a platform featuring training exercises and tools.

But when AJ wanted to get hyped for a 2021 fight, he turned to his musician cousin Maulo for some extra help. Maulo incorporated AJ's thoughts and emotions on fight night into the personalized walkout song "Ambition," which listeners can download from Spotify or Apple Music. Although AJ lost the 2021 fight to Ukrainian boxer Oleksandr Usyk, AJ looked forward to a rematch. As the "Ambition" lyrics say, "If I fail today/Tomorrow/I'll get a next chance."[3]

David Letterman did a parody of the ad, Under Armour knew it had a hit on its hands. Under Armour began airing two more ads, and the campaign's success resulted in more than 500,000 email and phone responses from consumers between 2003 and 2005.[2]

PROTECTING UNDER ARMOUR'S HOUSE

Under Armour had early success in part because it was an industry disrupter. Although its competitors had versions of moisture-management fabrics, Plank convinced athletes to help promote his idea of wearing his polyester-blend fabric as a base layer under their uniforms. This word-of-mouth approach helped him succeed. But management experts note that to continue thriving, disrupters must expand

and introduce new products that reach new audiences while at the same time protecting their existing business from copycat companies.

Adding apparel for women was one step Under Armour took to protect its own house. But the company's first attempt was a failure. In the early 2000s, Under Armour lost a large chunk of potential revenue when Plank decided the poor quality and fit of its new women's line meant those products couldn't be sold. After relying on more female designers and athletes, however, Under Armour was soon producing best-selling sports bras.

In 2005, Under Armour aired its first ad featuring a female athlete, US soccer team player Heather Mitts. In 2006, Under Armour brought in champion skier Lindsey Vonn to help expand the brand's

LINDSEY VONN BATTLES ON

Lindsey Vonn retired in 2019 as the greatest female ski racer ever. She won eight world championship medals, three Olympic medals, and a record 82 World Cup races. Since retiring, Vonn has joined other elite athletes such as Michael Phelps in advocating for mental health support.

Vonn, who has been an Under Armour endorser since 2006, joined forces with fellow endorser Dwayne "The Rock" Johnson in 2019 to help inspire athletes to push past obstacles. While introducing the Project Rock "Iron Will" collection, the company shared photos of her working out at Johnson's exclusive Iron Paradise gym. To inspire athletes to stay fit during the 2020 global pandemic, Under Armour also offered "Get Strong with Lindsey Vonn" workouts and healthy recipes.

appeal to women. At the time, 21-year-old Vonn made fun of Plank for following the industry's so-called "shrink it and pink it" approach of offering women a few smaller-sized men's products in pink. But Vonn came to believe the company did support female athletes and collaborated on her own line of Under Armour ski apparel in 2018.

In a continued effort to attract more female customers, Under Armour launched the "I Will What I Want" ad campaign in 2014, featuring ballerina Misty Copeland and model Gisele Bündchen, wife of superstar quarterback and Under Armour endorser Tom Brady. By 2016, women's products made up $1 billion of the company's $4.8 billion in sales.[4] In 2017, Under Armour continued its focus on women with its "Unlike Any" ad campaign, featuring such athletes as Copeland, Vonn, champion sprinter Natasha Hastings, and Paralympic track-and-field athlete Fleur Jong.

After these ad campaigns, Under Armour continued to diversify its outreach to its customers and the community. Its UA Freedom initiatives included the Department of Defense Warrior Games, an annual event in which hundreds of wounded military members and veterans competed in adaptive sporting events such as wheelchair

> *Copeland was one of the female athletes featured in Under Armour's women-focused "I Will What I Want" campaign.*

UNDER ARMOUR SHOWS ITS PRIDE

In 2016, a group of Under Armour's LGBTQ+ employees marched in the Baltimore Pride parade, sporting Under Armour–branded Pride shirts. The employees' idea to create these shirts eventually led to a consumer line of UA Pride products. In 2019, Under Armour added the rainbow-colored UA HOVR SLK EVO x Pride shoe to its collection in honor of the fiftieth anniversary of the Stonewall riots.

These 1969 riots occurred when police raided the popular New York City gay bar the Stonewall Inn. "This [wasn't] about commercializing a moment—it [was] about creating something real and authentic that will make a real impact on the community," explained Under Armour's SportStyle design director Katie Lau.[5] Proceeds from the collection benefit such groups as Athlete Ally, a nonprofit aimed at eliminating homophobia and transphobia in sports. Under Armour has also sponsored Pride parades in Baltimore; Austin, Texas; and New York City.

basketball. The competition celebrated the resilience of these military athletes.

In 2021, the company launched the Under Armour Pride collection, which includes apparel and shoes bearing sayings inspired by Pride Parade signs. Proceeds from the collection, whose development was led by LGBTQ+ members of Under Armour's workforce, helped support the Pride Center of Maryland in Baltimore, which advocates for the LGBTQ+ community.

CONNECTING ALL ATHLETES

Under Armour's "The Only Way Is Through" advertising campaign, launched in 2020, promoted some of its most prominent endorsers, including

> *In his work as an Under Armour brand ambassador, Phelps has talked about his ups and downs as a former Olympic athlete.*

Brady, Curry, Olympic champion swimmer Michael Phelps, and US soccer defender Kelley O'Hara. With this campaign, Under Armour also sought to inspire athletes at all levels to push past difficulties. In partnership with media company iHeart Radio, Under Armour released a "The Only Way Is Through" podcast, featuring interviews with elite athletes on their training, competition, and recovery routines.

    The company has also used its social media accounts to help athletes share inspiration. In 2021, Under Armour launched its "All Out Mile" challenge to spur runners to achieve their fastest mile run time within 30 days. Under

MICHAEL PHELPS

Phelps began representing Under Armour in 2010. But it was the company's 2016 "Rule Yourself" ad that Phelps said showed his real self to the public. The stark ad, created in honor of Phelps's final Olympics, hinted at how hard it was physically and mentally to become the world's most decorated Olympian with 28 medals. Phelps now promotes mental health awareness while sharing his own struggles and advice.

One way Phelps does this is through Under Armour's "The Only Way Is Through" campaign, launched in 2020 to help all athletes push past adversity. Phelps participated in the first iHeartRadio podcast for the campaign, telling listeners, "People thought I was absolutely crazy trying to win eight gold medals [at the 2008 Olympics]. I didn't . . . I visualized every little part of it."[6] Phelps also shares his visualization exercises through UA Performance Academy, a platform aimed at helping athletes strengthen their mental toughness.

Armour also made donations to youth charities and encouraged runners to share the event on social media to help promote youth sports.

Through its Instagram account, Under Armour promotes its "UA Sweat the Details" podcast. The podcast is intended to inspire athletes to reach their training goals. Under Armour's TikTok and Twitter feeds both feature videos of professional and amateur athletes training and competing. Sometimes on TikTok, customers just share fun videos of themselves in Under Armour apparel.

MENTAL TRAINING FOR ALL

In 2021, Under Armour launched its UA Performance Academy to share tips gleaned from its own human performance experts to help all athletes strengthen their mental health. These experts have studied how elite athletes respond when pushed to their mental and physical limits while doing activities such as snowshoeing at high altitude on Mount Hood in Oregon. They have learned that training athletes' minds to endure a challenge is just as important as training their bodies.

Through its Performance Academy platform, Under Armour provides mental strength exercises on such topics as goal setting, optimism, and resilience. Under Armour is also sharing the mental training journeys of elite athletes, including Phelps, WNBA Dallas Wings guard Bella Alarie, and Chinese Olympic volleyball champion Zhu Ting.

CHAPTER NINE

THE FUTURE OF UNDER ARMOUR

In 2021, Under Armour launched a new collection to celebrate its twenty-fifth anniversary. The collection includes several of the company's innovations produced since Under Armour was founded in 1996. The polo shirts feature the type of sweat-wicking fabric that first made Under Armour famous, and the shoes feature the UA HOVR cushioning technology the company introduced in 2018.

After a few difficult years, it seemed that Under Armour finally had cause to celebrate. In the spring of 2021, Under Armour reported that its North American sales had increased 32 percent, while its online sales were up 69 percent.[1] The previous

> *Under Armour has risen from a one-person company to one of today's largest sports brands.*

FITNESS GAMING

To help in reaching customers wherever they may be, Under Armour announced a partnership in 2021 with professional gamer Nick "NickMercs" Kolcheff. He has more than 13.5 million followers who not only watch him livestream video games but also follow his fitness tips. Through this partnership, Under Armour is investigating the potential of gaming to help athletes improve.

As a kid, Kolcheff participated in football, basketball, boxing, and arm wrestling while he was developing his interest in gaming. By his early teens, he was competing in video game tournaments across the United States. "Growing up, I always dreamed of a future where I could marry my passion for gaming with my commitment to compete at a high level in sports," said Kolcheff.[3]

year, Under Armour had taken steps to improve both of these figures.

FOLLOWING IN ITS COMPETITORS' FOOTSTEPS

Frisk announced plans in 2020 to start reducing the number of North American retail stores that sell Under Armour products by two to three thousand, with the goal of being in 10,000 stores by the end of 2022.[2] The move was Under Armour's attempt to gain more control over what it sells through retailers. Under Armour also owns stores where it sells its products directly to consumers. In North America, it has 18 Brand Houses, the stores where it sells its latest products, and 176 Factory Houses, where it sells older items at a discount.

In 2020, Under Armour also launched a new North American online shopping platform, with the goal of increasing the company's direct-to-consumer (DTC) sales. These steps have brought Under Armour's model closer to that of its competitors such as Nike, which now focuses more on its DTC business than its retail business. Like its competitors, Under Armour is trying to make it easier for customers to shop however they want, whether that means in stores or online.

Under Armour has been working to grow its global sales as well. The company has sold its products in more than 100 countries, including through its Brand and Factory Houses in Mexico and Chile. In 2021, the company introduced an online shopping platform in the Middle East. In 2020, international sales accounted

SPACE TRAVEL

When commercial astronauts fly with private space company Virgin Galactic, they'll be sporting Under Armour apparel. In 2019, Under Armour became the "technical spacewear partner" for Virgin Galactic. Under Armour designed custom space suits and footwear for Virgin Galactic pilots and passengers. The space suits include the company's UA Rush technology.

In 2020, Virgin Galactic also asked Under Armour to help make the seats more comfortable in the cabin of the VSS *Unity*, the spacecraft that launched Virgin Galactic founder Richard Branson and his crew into space in July 2021. Under Armour created a 3D knit fabric for the cabin seats. The fabric is designed to provide cushioning while allowing the seats to move to accommodate the intense forces of spaceflight.

▶ *International sales from stores such as this one in Malaysia have become an important and growing part of Under Armour's business.*

for about 31 percent of Under Armour's revenue. About 13 percent of its revenue came from the Europe/Middle East/Africa region.[4]

PRODUCTS AND PURPOSE

Like its competitors, Under Armour is always looking for ways to increase sales of its products. In 2020, also like its competitors, Under Armour put more focus on being a socially responsible company in the wake of economic and social justice issues that were amplified during the global pandemic. "Deepening our relationship with consumers also means living up to increasingly higher brand expectations," said Frisk in Under Armour's 2020 annual report.[5] Launching the Curry Brand was one step Under Armour took in 2020 to meet these expectations. Proceeds from the collection help fund youth sports in underserved communities.

Under Armour has also looked internally for ways to help address social issues. In 2020, the company launched internal employee discussions of anti-racism and racial justice issues. Under Armour has also set a goal of increasing the number of historically underrepresented employees in the company's leadership roles. In 2020, Under Armour's US employees at the director or above level were

LEVELING THE PLAYING FIELD

In 2021, Under Armour announced a partnership with the National Coalition of Minority Football Coaches to help find more long-term opportunities for minority coaches. The company noted that while more than 70 percent of NFL players in 2021 were people of color, only 16 percent of NFL coaches were people of color. This figure included only three Black head coaches.

The company committed to a five-year partnership to help change this and other disparities. Under Armour also noted that in college football, about 65 percent of players in 2021 were minorities, but only 15 percent of coaches were minorities.[6] Under Armour planned to provide funding to help prepare and promote minority coaches for open coaching positions.

78 percent white, 7 percent Hispanic, 7 percent Black, and 6 percent Asian.

Women are also lacking in leadership roles at Under Armour, and the company has set a goal of increasing their representation worldwide as well. In 2020, 37 percent of the director or above roles were filled by women. More than half of the company's global workforce is female, but Under Armour sought to have more women fill its commercial and technical roles.[7]

Under Armour has also examined its own operations to help address the global issue of climate change. In 2021, the company announced plans to change 80 percent of its facilities to use all renewable energy by 2025, with the goal of making this happen for 100 percent of its facilities by 2030. Under Armour also

TEAM PROGRESS

Under Armour set new diversity, equity, and inclusion (DEI) goals for the company in 2020. It had already aimed to increase the percentage of Black, Indigenous, and People of Color (BIPOC) individuals in higher-level positions from 22 to 30 percent. But the company added a goal of increasing the percentage of Black employees at this level from 8 to 12 percent by 2023.[8]

As part of its DEI efforts, Under Armour also has nine Teammate Resource Groups. These groups of employees work to promote culture and development across the company's workforce worldwide. Teams focus on a variety of communities, including women; Black, Latino, and Asian employees; LGBTQ+ employees; employees with diverse abilities; and veterans.

96

> *By shifting to using renewable energy at its facilities, Under Armour has aimed to become a greener company.*

declared it would strive to achieve net zero greenhouse gas emissions by 2050. As part of this effort, the company planned sustainable building design features for the new headquarters it planned to move into by 2025. "Earth is our home field. It's the only one we've got and we're going to protect it," Frisk said in the 2020 Under Armour annual report.[9]

AN OPTIMISTIC OUTLOOK

During the COVID-19 pandemic, Under Armour closed and then reopened a number of its Brand House and Factory stores. The retailers that carry Under Armour's products

> *By late 2021, customers were returning to Under Armour stores, and the company was on the road to recovery from the pandemic.*

did the same. Pandemic-related lockdowns in Vietnam, where Under Armour manufactures about one-third of its goods, affected supply.

By the fall of 2021, factories in places such as Vietnam had reopened, at least in a limited capacity. But Frisk said in November 2021 that Under Armour's biggest concern was getting those goods to consumers. Like many retailers, Under Armour was facing shipping delays and high shipping prices as part of the global supply chain issues that arose in 2021 as consumers' demand for goods skyrocketed. Frisk said Under Armour had often chosen the more expensive option of air freight to get around these issues.

Despite these challenges, Frisk also predicted that Under Armour would see a 25 percent increase in total sales from 2020.[10] This positive growth is a sign that Plank may have been right about his beliefs in the company's longevity. Plank said in 2019, "We are playing the long game, building an eternal brand."[11] Since its founding in 1996, Under Armour has become one of the biggest sports brands on Earth, and its leadership hopes to build on that incredible success.

ESSENTIAL FACTS

KEY EVENTS

- Kevin Plank starts Under Armour in 1996, focusing on sweat-wicking sports apparel.

- In 1999, Under Armour receives major public exposure when its apparel appears in the football film *Any Given Sunday*.

- In 2001, Under Armour inks its first major league deals with the National Hockey League and Major League Baseball.

- In 2005, chief executive officer (CEO) Kevin Plank takes Under Armour public.

- Under Armour surpasses $1 billion in sales in 2010.

- In 2017, chief operating officer Patrik Frisk works to reverse declining sales.

- Frisk becomes the CEO of Under Armour in 2020, and Plank's role changes to executive chairman and brand chief.

- In 2021, after sales begin to recover from their pandemic dip, Frisk predicts a 25 percent increase in revenue in 2022.

KEY PEOPLE

- Kevin Plank founds Under Armour in 1996 and serves as chief executive officer (CEO) through 2019.

- Under Armour signs Olympic champion skier Lindsey Vonn in 2006, in part to help attract more female customers.

- Superstar quarterback Tom Brady becomes Under Armour's highest-profile brand ambassador in 2010.

- Patrik Frisk joins Under Armour in 2017 as chief operating officer and becomes CEO in 2020.

- Under Armour works with Golden State Warriors star guard Stephen Curry to introduce his Curry Brand in 2020 as part of an increased company focus on helping fund youth sports.

KEY PRODUCTS

- The Shorty: Kevin Plank starts Under Armour in 1996 with this sweat-wicking T-shirt, the company's first HeatGear product.

- ColdGear: Under Armour expands its performance apparel product line in 1997 with a fabric designed to circulate body heat while wicking away moisture.

- Performance Underwear: Under Armour introduces its first line of sweat-wicking underwear in 2002, adding the Armour Bra in 2012.

- Connected Footwear: In 2016, Under Armour releases its first running shoes that use a sensor to digitally track athletes' performance.

- HOVR technology: Under Armour works with Dow Chemical to introduce the UA HOVR sneaker in 2018; the shoe uses a proprietary cushioning foam compound.

QUOTE

"We are playing the long game, building an eternal brand."

—Under Armour founder and former CEO Kevin Plank

GLOSSARY

accolade
An award in honor of an achievement.

aerodynamics
The factors that affect how air flows around an object.

alma mater
The school from which someone has graduated.

ambassador
An individual authorized by an organization or company to represent it or its products.

analyst
Someone who studies a company's financial information.

apparel
Clothing.

disrupter
A company that uses innovation to change an industry.

innovative
Having original new methods and features.

net proceeds
The amount of money earned from a sale after costs are subtracted.

posthumously
Occurring after someone has died.

proprietary
Created by someone who has an exclusive legal right to use it.

prototype
A single sample of a prospective product used to show potential customers and investors to gauge their interest.

restructuring
Changing how a company does business when it's in financial trouble.

revenue
The money a company takes in.

sensor
A device that detects or measures a physical property.

stock
A portion of a company's value that people can buy and sell.

sustainable
Meeting current needs without harming the ability of future generations to meet their needs.

trade show
A private event at which companies in an industry display their products.

ADDITIONAL RESOURCES

SELECTED BIBLIOGRAPHY

Dessauer, Carin. "Team Player: For Under Armour CEO and Kensington Native Kevin Plank, It's Always Been about the Huddle." *Bethesda Magazine*, 1 Mar. 2009, bethesdamagazine.com. Accessed 25 Nov. 2021.

Hobein, Dennis. "After a Year of Rehab, Under Armour Is Poised for a Major Comeback." *Motley Fool*, 21 June 2021, fool.com. Accessed 25 Nov. 2021.

Mirabella, Lorraine, and Lillian Reed. "Who Is New Under Armour CEO Patrik Frisk?" *Baltimore Sun*, 22 Oct. 2019, baltimoresun.com. Accessed 25 Nov. 2021.

FURTHER READINGS

Harris, Duchess, JD, PhD, and Michael Miller. *Race and Sports Management*. Abdo, 2019.

Mooney, Carla. *Nike*. Abdo, 2023.

Scheff, Matt. *Excelling in Football*. ReferencePoint, 2020.

ONLINE RESOURCES

To learn more about Under Armour, please visit **abdobooklinks.com** or scan this QR code. These links are routinely monitored and updated to provide the most current information available.

MORE INFORMATION

For more information on this subject, contact or visit the following organizations:

GOOD SPORTS

1515 Washington St., Ste. 300
Braintree, MA 02184
617-471-1213
goodsports.org

Under Armour partners with Good Sports, an organization that seeks to give youths equitable access to sports and athletic activities.

UNDER ARMOUR

1020 Hull St.
Baltimore, MD 21230
1-888-727-6687
about.underarmour.com/about

Under Armour's website includes information about the company's history, its current product line, and its latest technological innovations.

SOURCE NOTES

CHAPTER 1. UNDER ARMOUR REBOUNDS

1. Dennis Hobein. "After a Year of Rehab, Under Armour Is Poised for a Major Comeback." *Motley Fool*, 21 June 2021, fool.com. Accessed 3 Mar. 2022.

2. "2020 Annual Report." *Under Armour*, 26 Mar. 2021, underarmour.com. Accessed 3 Mar. 2022.

3. Paolo Songco. "Warriors' Stephen Curry Reveals Hilarious Backstory behind Dumping Nike, Adidas in Favor of Under Armour." *ClutchPoints*, 19 May 2021, clutchpoints.com. Accessed 3 Mar. 2022.

CHAPTER 2. IT STARTED WITH SWEAT

1. Carin Dessauer. "Team Player." *Bethesda Magazine*, 1 Mar. 2009, bethesdamagazine.com. Accessed 3 Mar. 2022.

2. J. D. Harrison. "When We Were Small: Under Armour." *Washington Post*, 12 Nov. 2014, washingtonpost.com. Accessed 3 Mar. 2022.

3. P. Smith. "Total Revenue of the Global Sports Apparel Market from 2021 to 2028." *Statista*, 23 Feb. 2022, statista.com. Accessed 3 Mar. 2022.

4. P. Smith. "Sales of the Biggest Athletic Apparel, Accessories, and Footwear Companies Worldwide in 2019/20." *Statista*, 13 Jan. 2022, statista.com. Accessed 3 Mar. 2022.

5. Dessauer, "Team Player."

6. Harrison, "When We Were Small."

7. Dessauer, "Team Player."

8. "Why Did Under Armour CEO Kevin Plank Send Christmas Cards to Nike?" *Today*, 23 June 2017, today.com. Accessed 3 Mar. 2022.

9. Kevin Lynch. "Under Armour Reveals Plans for New 4 Million Sq. Ft. Port Covington Campus." *South Bmore*, 28 Jan. 2016, southbmore.com. Accessed 3 Mar. 2022.

10. Lynch, "Under Armour Reveals Plans."

CHAPTER 3. A BIG BREAK ON THE BIG SCREEN

1. "Any Given Sunday." *IMDB*, n.d., imdb.com. Accessed 3 Mar. 2022.

2. David Claxton. "How Under Armour Used 'Any Given Sunday' to Take on Nike & Adidas." *Business of Sport*, 11 Apr. 2017, businessofsport.net. Accessed 3 Mar. 2022.

3. "Our Story." *Under Armour*, n.d., about.underarmour.com. Accessed 3 Mar. 2022.

4. Claxton, "How Under Armour Used 'Any Given Sunday.'"

5. "#9 Tom Brady." *Forbes*, 4 June 2021, forbes.com. Accessed 3 Mar. 2022.

6. "Under Armour Startup Story." *Fundable*, n.d., fundable.com. Accessed 3 Mar. 2022.

7. "Under Armour on Inc. 600." *Under Armour*, 1 Dec. 2003, investor.underarmour.com. Accessed 3 Mar. 2022.

8. "Kevin Plank—Fast 50 2003." *Fast Company*, 28 Feb. 2003, fastcompany.com. Accessed 3 Mar. 2022.

9. "Under Armour Reports 2005 Fourth Quarter and Full Year Results and Provides Outlook for 2006." *Under Armour*, 7 Feb. 2006, uabiz.com. Accessed 3 Mar. 2022.

10. "Our Story."

11. "Our Story."

12. Stuart Elliot. "'Regular' Underwear? Under Armour Says It's a Cut Above." *New York Times*, 30 Apr. 2012, nytimes.com. Accessed 3 Mar. 2022.

CHAPTER 4. RISE, FALL, AND RISE AGAIN

1. "Under Armour Revenue 2010–2021." *Macrotrends*, n.d., macrotrends.net. Accessed 3 Mar. 2022.

2. "Under Armour Shares Under Fire over Speed Skating Suits." *CNBC*, 14 Feb. 2014, cnbc.com. Accessed 3 Mar. 2022.

3. Dennis Hobein. "After a Year of Rehab, Under Armour Is Poised for a Major Comeback." *Motley Fool*, 21 June 2021, fool.com. Accessed 3 Mar. 2022.

4. Dennis Green. "A Massive Shift in American Fashion Is Causing a $1.3 Billion Problem for Under Armour." *Insider*, 26 July 2018, businessinsider.com. Accessed 3 Mar. 2022.

5. "Athleisure Market Report 2021." *Businesswire*, 11 Aug. 2021, businesswire.com. Accessed 3 Mar. 2022.

6. "2020 Annual Report." *Under Armour*, 26 Mar. 2021, underarmour.com. Accessed 3 Mar. 2022.

7. Hobein, "After a Year of Rehab, Under Armour Is Poised for a Major Comeback."

8. Holden Wilen. "Under Armour Agrees to Pay $9M to Settle SEC Accounting Probe." *Baltimore Business Journal*, 3 May 2021, bizjournals.com. Accessed 3 Mar. 2022.

9. Lorraine Mirabella. "Under Armour Makes Case That Its Turnaround Plan Is Working—Though Some Analysts Are Still Skeptical." *Baltimore Sun*, 12 Dec. 2018, baltimoresun.com. Accessed 3 Mar. 2022.

10. "Patrik Frisk to Become Chief Executive Officer of Under Armour on January 1, 2020." *Under Armour*, 22 Oct. 2019, about.underarmour.com. Accessed 3 Mar. 2022.

11. Shoshy Ciment and Mary Hanbury. "Here's How Under Armour Went from a New Hotshot Sportswear Brand Taking on Nike to Having a Wholly Uncertain Future." *Business Insider*, 9 Sept. 2020, businessinsider.com. Accessed 3 Mar. 2022.

12. Darrell Etherington. "Under Armour to Sell MyFitnessPal for $345 Million, after Acquiring It in 2015 for $475 Million." *TechCrunch*, 30 Oct. 2020, techcrunch.com. Accessed 3 Mar. 2022.

13. Hobein, "After a Year of Rehab, Under Armour Is Poised for a Major Comeback."

14. "As Young Athletes Struggle to Compete During Pandemic, Under Armour Makes Sure They Can Still Play Responsibly." *Under Armour*, 6 Oct. 2020, about.underarmour.com. Accessed 3 Mar. 2022.

CHAPTER 5. UNDER ARMOUR INNOVATIONS

1. "2020 Annual Report." *Under Armour*, 26 Mar. 2021, underarmour.com. Accessed 3 Mar. 2022.

2. Jamie Smith Hopkins. "Perspiration Led to Plank's Inspiration." *Baltimore Sun*, 26 Aug. 2005, baltimoresun.com. Accessed 3 Mar. 2022.

3. David Kiley. "Under Armour Steps into Footwear Field." *NBC News*, 31 Jan. 2008, nbcnews.com. Accessed 3 Mar. 2022.

4. Kiley, "Under Armour Steps into Footwear Field."

5. J. D. Harrison. "When We Were Small: Under Armour." *Washington Post*, 12 Nov. 2014, washingtonpost.com. Accessed 3 Mar. 2022.

6. "Under Armour Unveils Its Fastest Performance Running Shoe Yet." *Under Armour*, 12 Feb. 2021, about.underarmour.com. Accessed 3 Mar. 2022.

7. "Going with a New Flow." *Under Armour*, 4 Dec. 2020, about.underarmour.com. Accessed 3 Mar. 2022.

8. "Let's Connect." *Under Armour*, 8 Nov. 2018, about.underarmour.com. Accessed 3 Mar. 2022.

9. "Run Coaching in UA HOVR Proven to Improve Athlete Performance." *Under Armour*, 28 Jan. 2021, about.underarmour.com. Accessed 3 Mar. 2022.

SOURCE NOTES CONTINUED

CHAPTER 6. POWERING COLLEGE AND PRO ATHLETES

1. Edward Lee. "Under Armour and University of Maryland Say They Remain Committed to Each Other." *Baltimore Sun*, 6 Nov. 2019, baltimoresun.com. Accessed 3 Mar. 2022.

2. Lee, "Under Armour and University of Maryland Say They Remain Committed to Each Other."

3. "For Natasha Hastings, the Right Mindset Makes All the Difference." *Under Armour*, 10 Mar. 2021, about.underarmour.com. Accessed 3 Mar. 2022.

4. Holden Wilen. "Under Armour Cuts Its Sponsorship Commitments in Half." *Baltimore Business Journal*, 25 Feb. 2021, bizjournals.com. Accessed 3 Mar. 2022.

5. Jessica Golden. "Under Armour Delaying Payments to Some of Its Athletes as It Deals with the Fallout from Coronavirus." *CNBC*, 12 May 2020, cnbc.com. Accessed 3 Mar. 2022.

6. Jenna West. "Report: Nike to Supply MLB Uniforms Instead of Under Armour." *Sports Illustrated*, 24 May 2018, si.com. Accessed 3 Mar. 2022.

7. Rob Lenihan. "Under Armour Ends NFL Licensing Deal Days Ahead of Super Bowl." *TheStreet*, 3 Feb. 2021, thestreet.com. Accessed 3 Mar. 2022.

8. Joe Levy. "Trent Alexander-Arnold Signs Under Armour Boot Deal." *Sports Pro Media*, 22 Mar. 2019, sportspromedia.com. Accessed 3 Mar. 2022.

9. "Pink Is the Color We Can All Root For." *Under Armour*, 29 Oct. 2021, about.underarmour.com. Accessed 3 Mar. 2022.

10. Holden Wilen. "Under Armour, University of Cincinnati Agree to Buyout of $50M Sponsorship Deal." *Baltimore Business Journal*, 18 Nov. 2020, bizjournals.com. Accessed 3 Mar. 2022.

11. Wilen, "Under Armour, University of Cincinnati Agree to Buyout of $50M Sponsorship Deal."

12. Mark Schlabach. "UCLA Sues Under Armour for Terminating $280 Million Sponsorship Deal with School." *ESPN*, 26 Aug. 2020, espn.com. Accessed 3 Mar. 2022.

13. Malathi Nayak. "Under Armour Can't Escape UCLA Suit Over Sports Sponsorship Deal." *Bloomberg*, 26 Aug. 2021, bloomberg.com. Accessed 3 Mar. 2022.

14. Max Zahn with Andy Serwer. "Under Armour Sees 'Lots of Opportunities' in College Athlete Endorsements: CEO." *Yahoo Finance*, 2 Sept. 2021, news.yahoo.com. Accessed 3 Mar. 2022.

CHAPTER 7. SUPPORTING YOUTH ATHLETES

1. "2021 Foundation Spotlight: Under Armour." *Cal Ripken, Sr. Foundation*, 2020, ripkenfoundation.org. Accessed 3 Mar. 2022.

2. "UA Teammate Runs Ultra Marathon to Raise Money to Support Every Kid Sports." *Under Armour*, 16 Sept. 2021, about.underarmour.com. Accessed 3 Mar. 2022.

3. "UA Teammate Runs Ultra Marathon to Raise Money to Support Every Kid Sports."

4. "Ready for Anything." *Under Armour*, 10 Sept. 2020, about.underarmour.com. Accessed 3 Mar. 2022.

5. "ESPN, Under Armour and LISC Announce New Round of Funding to Transform Vacant Spaces into Valuable Places for Sports, Recreation, and Play." *LISC*, 7 Dec. 2020, lisc.org. Accessed 3 Mar. 2022.

6. "UA Building Bridges Through Basketball." *Under Armour*, 10 July 2019, about.underarmour.com. Accessed 3 Mar. 2022.

7. "UA Building Bridges Through Basketball."

8. "2021 Women's History Month." *Under Armour*, n.d., impact.underarmour.com. Accessed 3 Mar. 2022.

9. "Building Future Leaders Through a Commitment to Girls Sports." *Under Armour*, 3 Mar. 2021, about.underarmour.com. Accessed 3 Mar. 2022.

10. "Baltimore Ravens & Under Armour Announce New Partnership." *CBS Baltimore*, 8 Oct. 2021, baltimore.cbslocal.com. Accessed 3 Mar. 2022.

11. "Building Future Leaders Through a Commitment to Girls Sports."

12. "Celebrating Veterans: Stronger Communities Are Built on the Bedrock of Personal Character." *Under Armour*, 11 Nov. 2021, about.underarmour.com. Accessed 3 Mar. 2022.

CHAPTER 8. MARKETING AND MESSAGING

1. "Our Story." *Under Armour*, n.d., about.underarmour.com. Accessed 3 Mar. 2022.

2. "Under Armour Launches Third Installment of 'Protect This House' TV Ad Trilogy." *Under Armour*, 15 Sept. 2005, about.underarmour.com. Accessed 3 Mar. 2022.

3. "Anthony Joshua Teams Up with Musician Maulo for Personalized Fight Night Song." *Under Armour*, 19 Aug. 2021, about.underarmour.com. Accessed 3 Mar. 2022.

4. Jeff Barker. "Under Armour's Challenge: Reaching Women." *Baltimore Sun*, 4 Aug. 2017, baltimoresun.com. Accessed 3 Mar. 2022.

5. "Unified with Pride." *Under Armour*, 3 June 2019, about.underarmour.com. Accessed 3 Mar. 2022.

6. "Michael Phelps: Fish Out of Water." *iHeart: The Only Way Is Through Podcast*, 23 July 2020, iheart.com. Accessed 3 Mar. 2022.

CHAPTER 9. THE FUTURE OF UNDER ARMOUR

1. "Under Armour Reports First Quarter 2021 Results; Raised Full Year Outlook." *Under Armour*, 4 May 2021, about.underarmour.com. Accessed 3 Mar. 2022.

2. Joe Keenan. "Under Armour to Exit Up to 3,000 Wholesale Doors." *TotalRetail*, 2 Nov. 2020, mytotalretail.com. Accessed 3 Mar. 2022.

3. "Getting Better Together." *Under Armour*, 4 Aug. 2021, about.underarmour.com. Accessed 3 Mar. 2022.

4. "2020 Annual Report." *Under Armour*, 26 Mar. 2021, underarmour.com. Accessed 3 Mar. 2022.

5. "2020 Annual Report."

6. "Level the Playing Field." *Under Armour*, 9 Nov. 2021, about.underarmour.com. Accessed 3 Mar. 2022.

7. "2020 Annual Report."

8. "Diversity, Equity, and Inclusion." *Under Armour*, n.d., about.underarmour.com. Accessed 3 Mar. 2022.

9. "2020 Annual Report."

10. Lauren Thomas. "Under Armour Shares Soar as Earnings Beat Prompts Retailer to Hike Annual Outlook." *CNBC*, 2 Nov. 2021, cnbc.com. Accessed 3 Mar. 2022.

11. "Celebrating 25 Years of Under Armour." *Under Armour*, 1 July 2021, about.underarmour.com. Accessed 3 Mar. 2022.

INDEX

Adidas, 17
advertising, 28, 43, 81, 86
Alexander-Arnold, Trent, 63
AllSeasonGear, 21, 23, 28, 48
Any Given Sunday, 25–29
athleisure, 37, 41

Baltimore, Maryland, 10, 21, 22, 26, 53, 71, 77, 86
basketball, 5–10, 12, 21, 74–75, 79, 86, 92
Black Lives Matter, 63
Brady, Tom, 28, 62, 84, 87
Brand Houses, 27, 32, 92, 97
Building Bridges through Basketball (BBTB), 74–76

Cal Ripken Sr. Foundation, 71–72
charity, 10, 12, 27, 43, 60, 72–74, 77, 79, 83, 88
ColdGear, 21, 28, 48, 49
company name, 18–19
compression shorts, 15–16
connected footwear, 43, 53, 55, 69
Copeland, Misty, 9, 84
cotton, 15, 16–17, 47, 48
COVID-19 pandemic, 12–13, 21, 37–38, 42–43, 61–62, 66, 73, 83, 95, 97
Curry, Stephen, 10–11, 13, 39–40, 54, 73, 87

diversity, equity, and inclusion (DEI), 96
Dow Chemical, 53–54, 68

ESPN, 18, 27, 29, 51, 73–74

Factory Houses, 92–93
Foxx, Jamie, 26–27
Frisk, Patrik, 13, 40–42, 47, 56, 67, 92, 95, 97–99
Fulks, Kip, 20, 22

Georgia Tech, 18, 48, 59
Girls Opportunity Alliance, 77
Grimes, Troy, 72

Harper, Bryce, 61
Hastings, Natasha, 60, 73, 84
headquarters, 21, 22, 53, 54, 97
HeatGear, 21, 28, 48
Holcombe Rucker Park, 12
HOVR shoes, 9, 53, 55–56, 61, 68–69, 86, 91

international sales, 93–94

Johnson, Dwayne "The Rock," 26, 27, 79, 83
Joshua, Anthony, 73, 82

Knight, Phil, 21
Kolcheff, Nick "NickMercs," 92

Letterman, David, 82
Lighthouse, 53
Lockheed Martin, 44, 51
Lululemon Athletica, 17, 37

Major League Baseball (MLB), 28, 61, 62, 71–72
Mitts, Heather, 83
movies, 25–27, 29
MyFitnessPal, 43

National Football League (NFL), 28, 32, 33, 49, 51, 62–63, 95
National Football League (NFL) Europe, 20
National Hockey League (NHL), 28
Nike, 13, 17, 20–21, 38, 67, 93

Obama, Michelle, 77
Ogbogu, Eric, 49, 81
Olympics, 36, 44–45, 51, 60, 66, 73, 83, 87, 88, 89
online shopping, 38, 43, 91, 93

Performance Academy, 82, 88–89
Phelps, Michael, 83, 87, 88, 89
Plank, Kevin, 15–22, 25–26, 30–31, 39–40, 41, 47–49, 51, 59–60, 81–84, 99
podcasts, 87–88
"Protect This House," 81
Prototype shoes, 49–50
Puma, 17

Quinn, Brendan, 15

RePlay initiative, 74

Securities and Exchange Commission (SEC), 39
Shorty T-shirt, 21, 47, 48
softball, 66
speedskating, 36, 44–45, 51
Spieth, Jordan, 30
Stone, Oliver, 25–26

"The Only Way Is Through," 42, 43, 86–87, 88
3D printed shoes, 53
Travis Manion Foundation (TMF), 78–79

UA Flow Velociti Wind, 56
UA Next, 79
Under Armour Pride collection, 86
underwear, 33
University of California, Berkeley, 64
University of California, Los Angeles (UCLA), 65–66
University of Cincinnati, 63
University of Maryland, 15, 17–18, 19, 51, 59–60, 81
University of Minnesota Duluth, 60–61
University of Notre Dame, 35

Virgin Galactic, 93
Vonn, Lindsey, 83–84

wicking material, 5, 16–17, 23, 33, 47, 48, 49, 91
Women's History Month, 76
Workout, The, 18

ABOUT THE AUTHOR

SARAH ROGGIO

Sarah Roggio lives in Chicago, Illinois, where she loves to sail on Lake Michigan with her husband. She is a graduate of Northwestern University's Medill School of Journalism.

ABOUT THE CONSULTANTS

DR. ANTONIO S. WILLIAMS

Dr. Antonio S. Williams is a native of Swansea, South Carolina, and currently lives in Indianapolis, Indiana, with his wife, Crystal, and their three children, AJ, Anderson, and Ava. Dr. Williams is an associate professor in the School of Public Health at Indiana University Bloomington, where he serves as associate department chair, director of graduate studies, and director of sport management within the department of kinesiology. As a leading scholar in sport branding, Williams has been a board member for the American Council on Exercise, a player brand strategist for the Indianapolis Colts, a brand strategist for Indiana University Athletics, and a former member of the 2012 Super Bowl Host Committee. He has been featured and quoted in media outlets such as the *New York Times*, Fox News, the *Washington Post*, and the *Chicago Tribune*. He has published more than 80 scholarly works on sport and fitness branding.

ZACK P. PEDERSEN

Zack P. Pedersen lives in Bloomington, Indiana, with his wife, Megan, and is currently a PhD student in the sport management program at Indiana University Bloomington. His primary research focus is the creation, utilization, and advancement of athlete brands through various branding strategies.